PEMMICAN
A Girl Called ECHO
VOL. I

By Katherena Vermette
Illustrated by Scott B. Henderson
Coloured by Donovan Yaciuk

HIGHWATER
PRESS

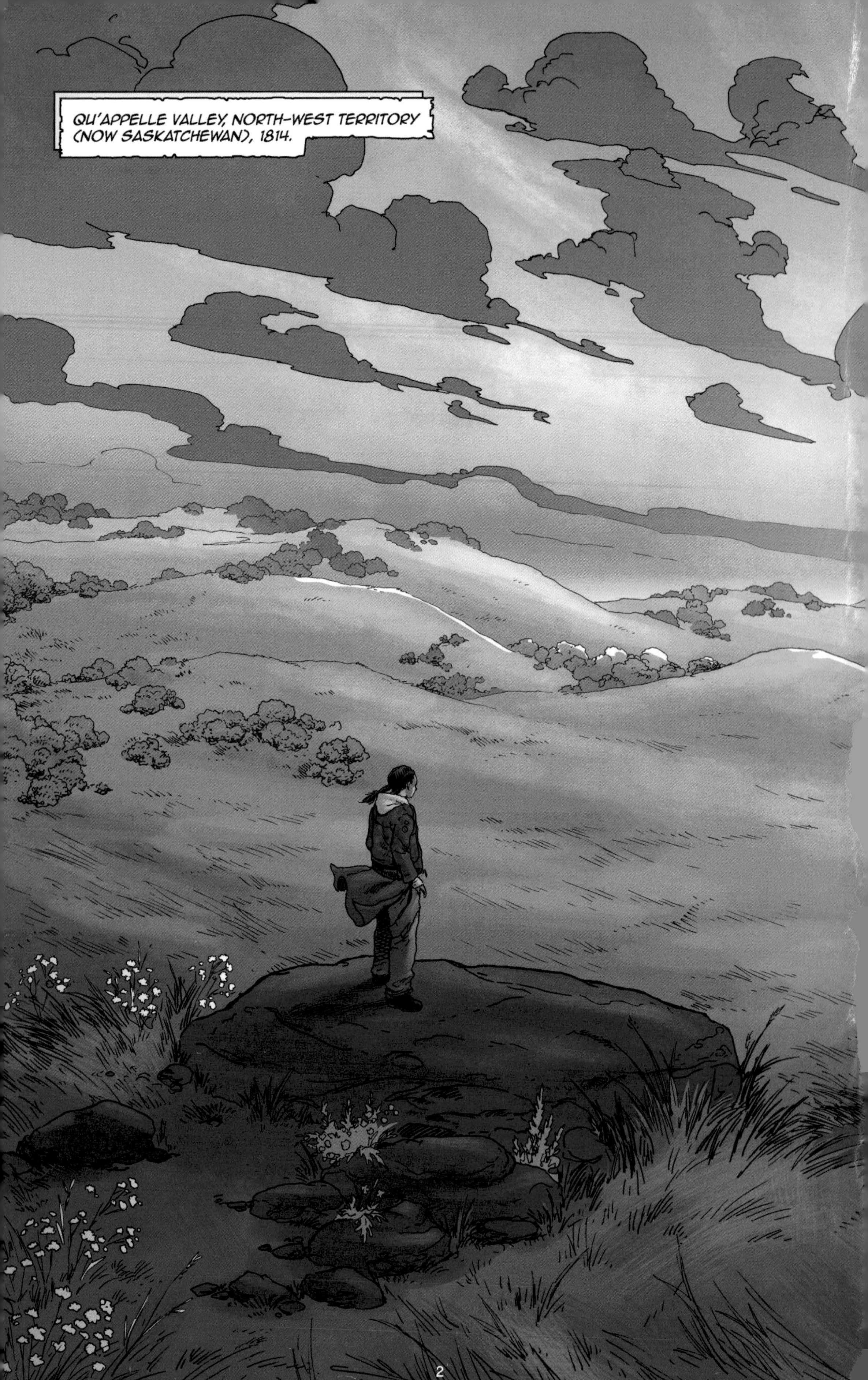
QU'APPELLE VALLEY, NORTH-WEST TERRITORY (NOW SASKATCHEWAN), 1814.

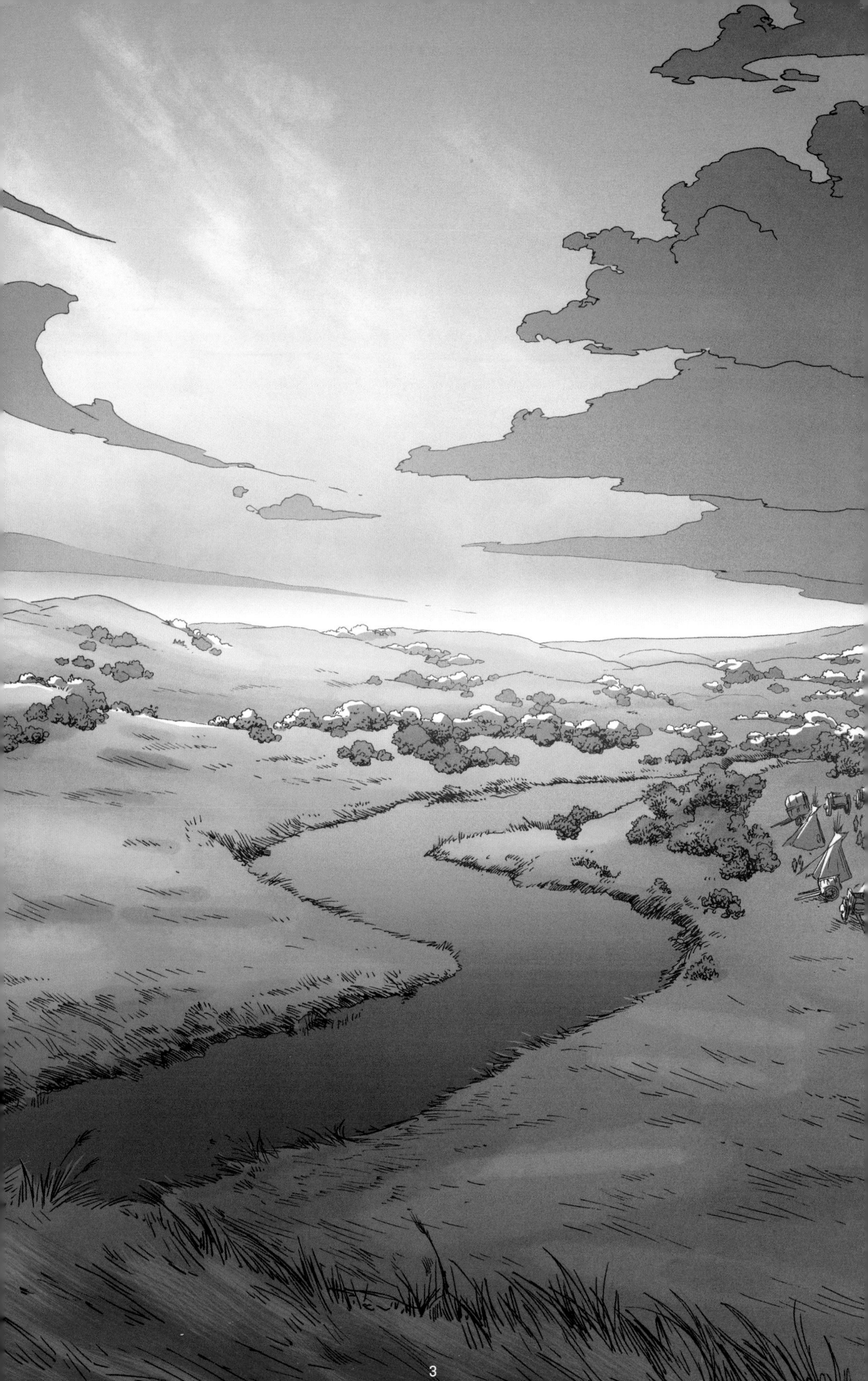

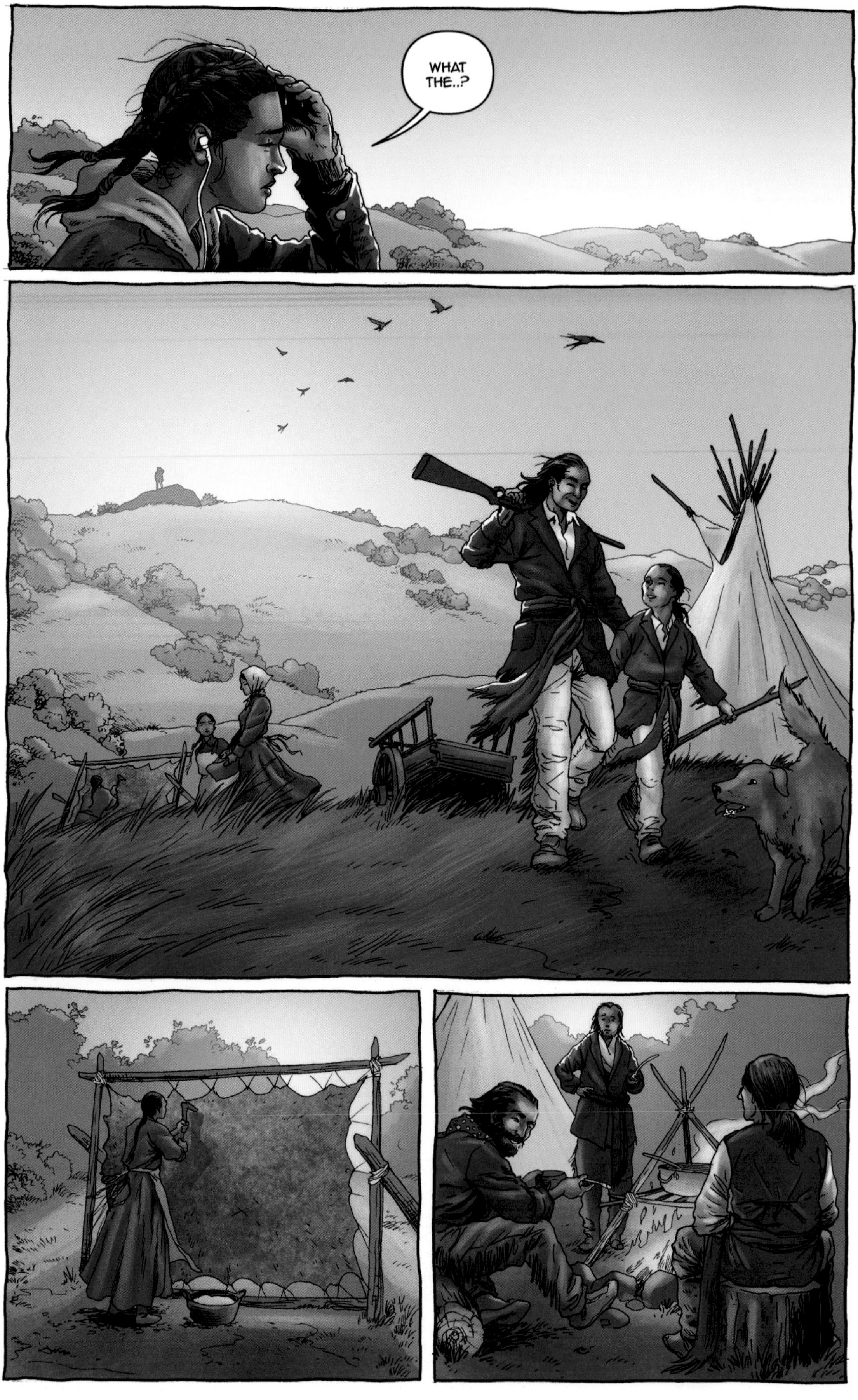
WHAT THE..?

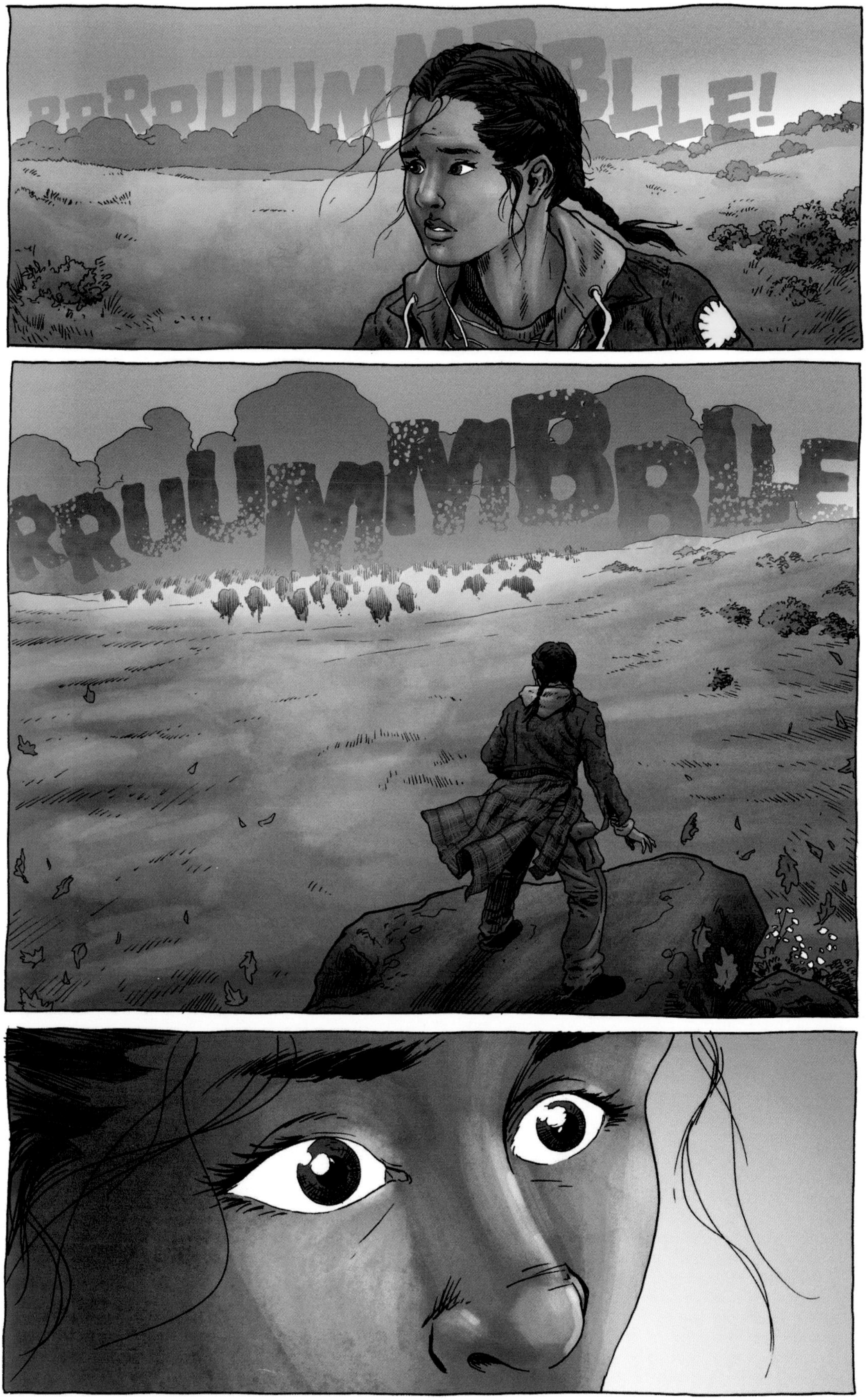
RRRRUUMMBBLLE!
RRUUMMBBLLE

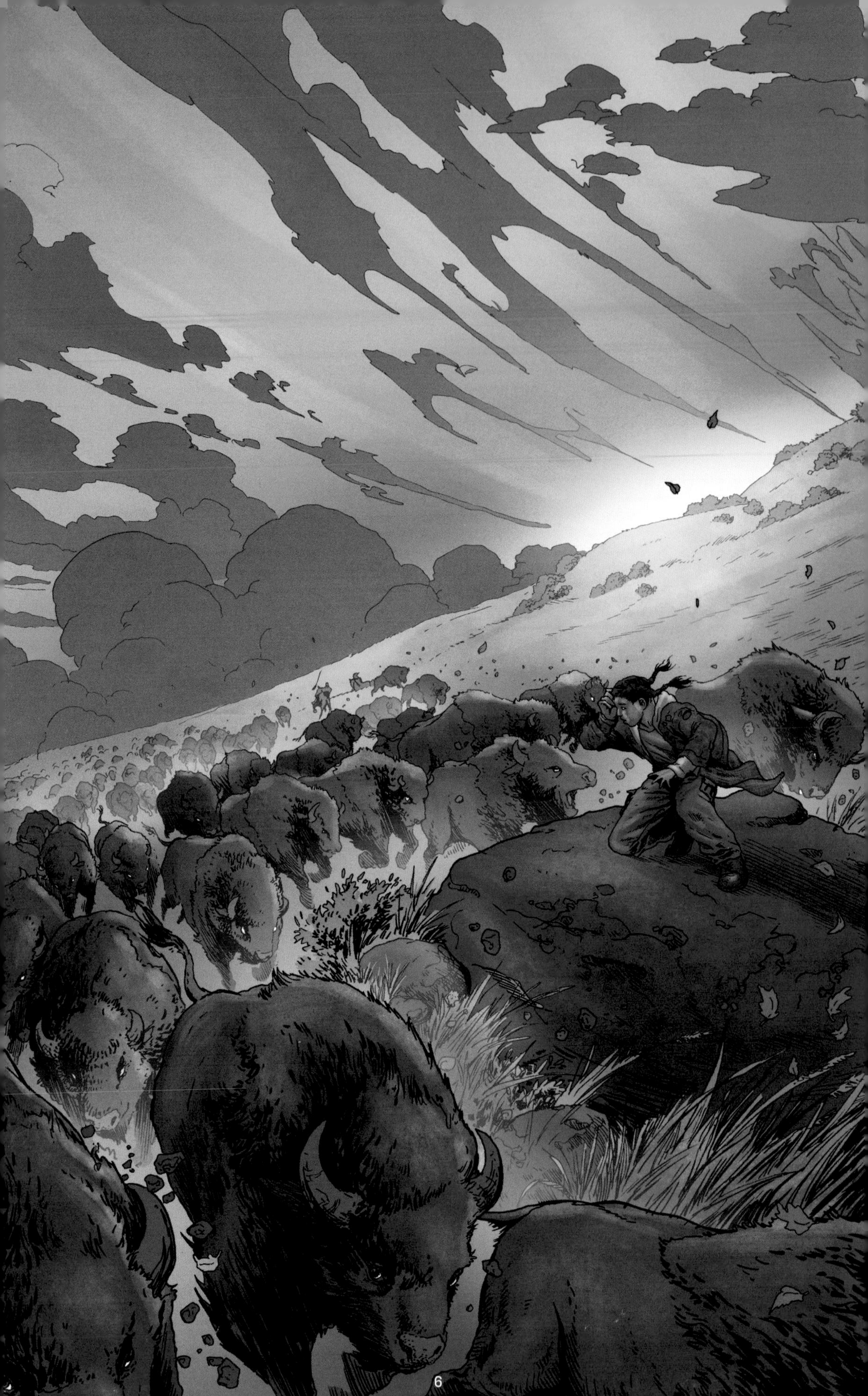

KA-BOOM!

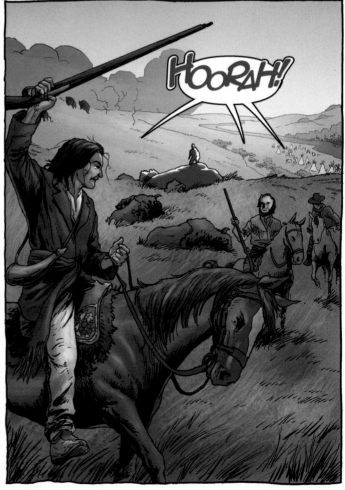

HOORAH!!

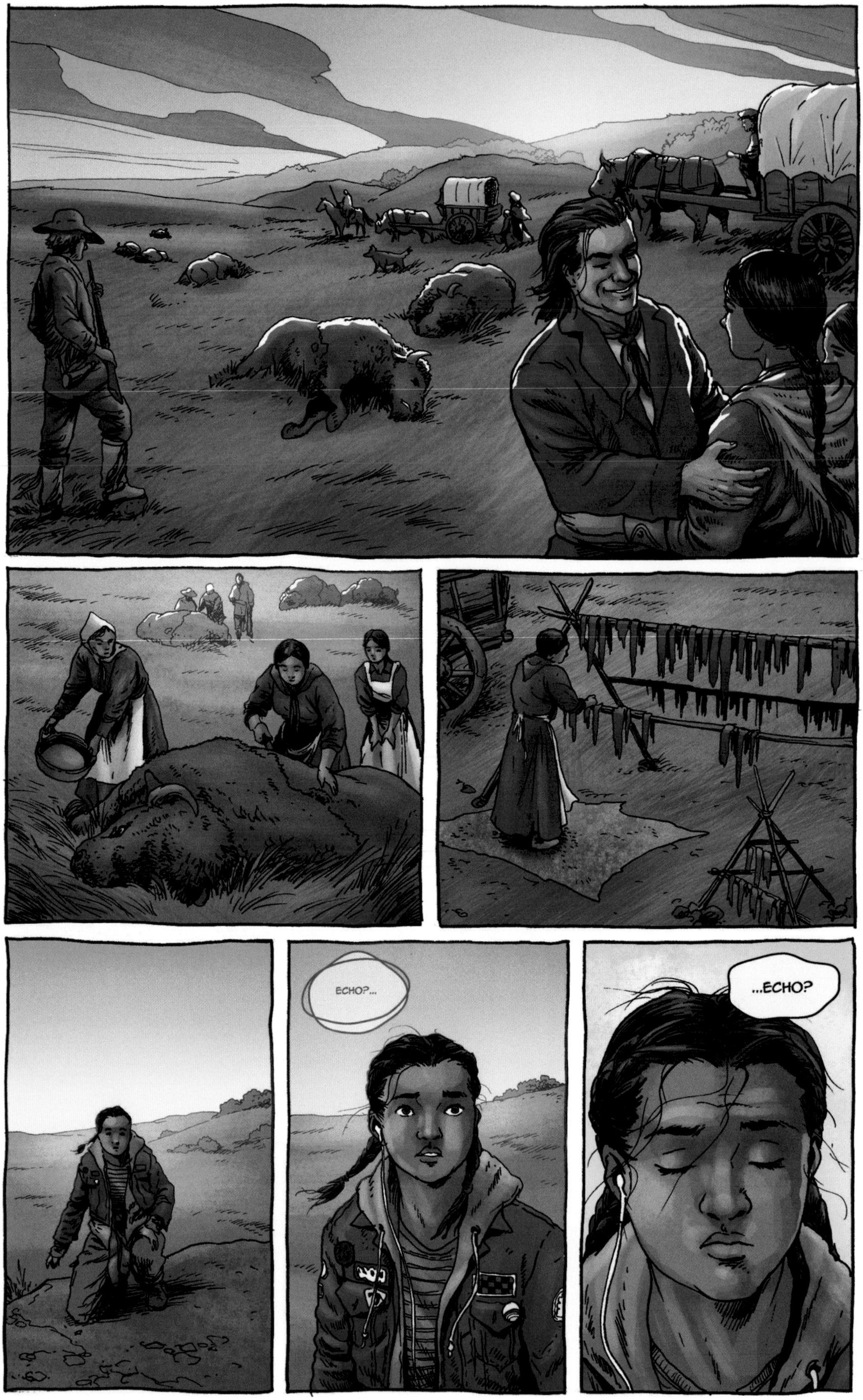
ECHO?...
...ECHO?

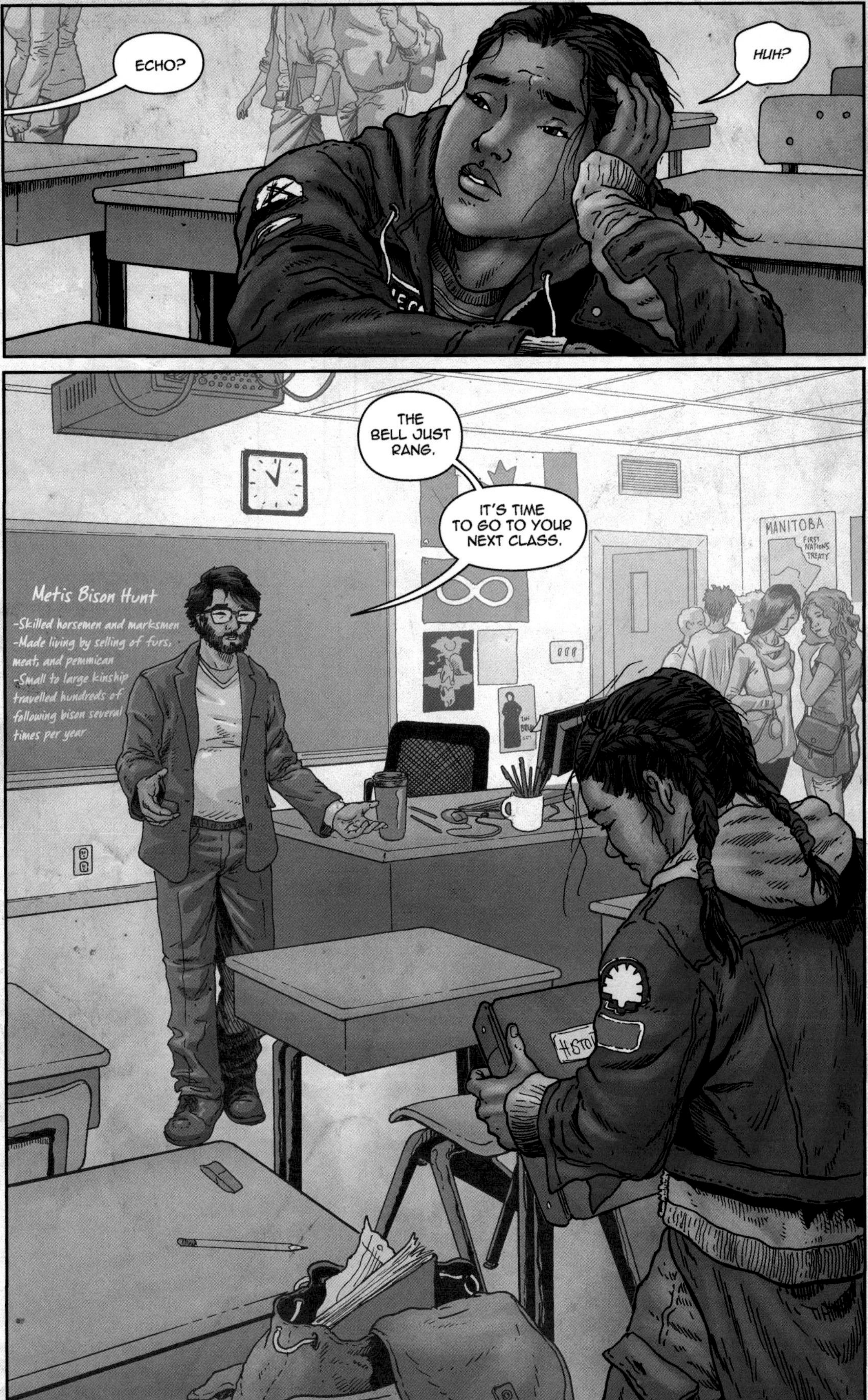
ECHO?
HUH?
THE BELL JUST RANG.
IT'S TIME TO GO TO YOUR NEXT CLASS.
Metis Bison Hunt
-Skilled horsemen and marksmen
-Made living by selling of furs, meat, and pemmican
-Small to large kinship travelled hundreds of following bison several times per year
MANITOBA
FIRST NATIONS TREATY

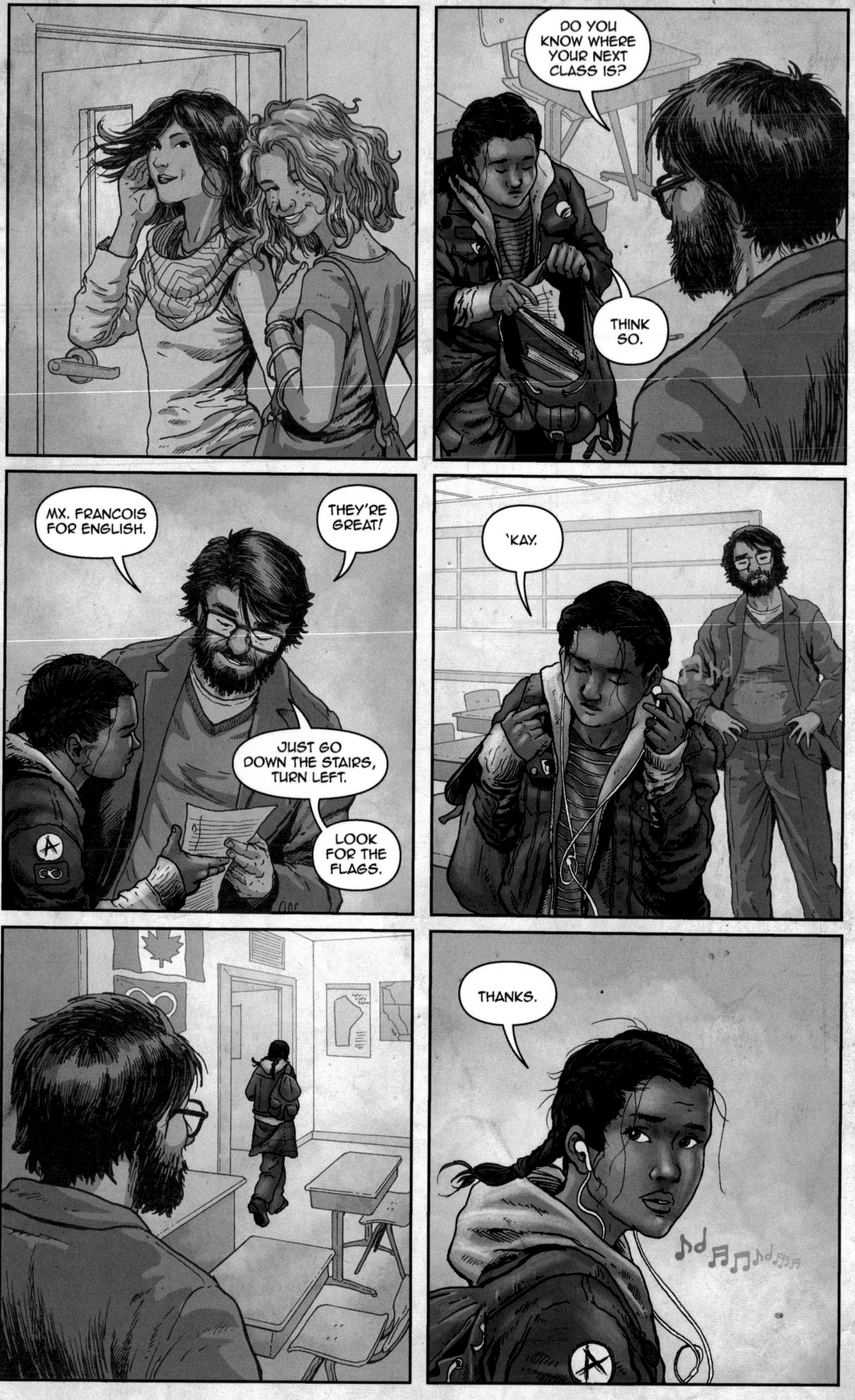
DO YOU KNOW WHERE YOUR NEXT CLASS IS?
THINK SO.
MX. FRANCOIS FOR ENGLISH.
THEY'RE GREAT!
JUST GO DOWN THE STAIRS, TURN LEFT.
LOOK FOR THE FLAGS.
'KAY.
THANKS.

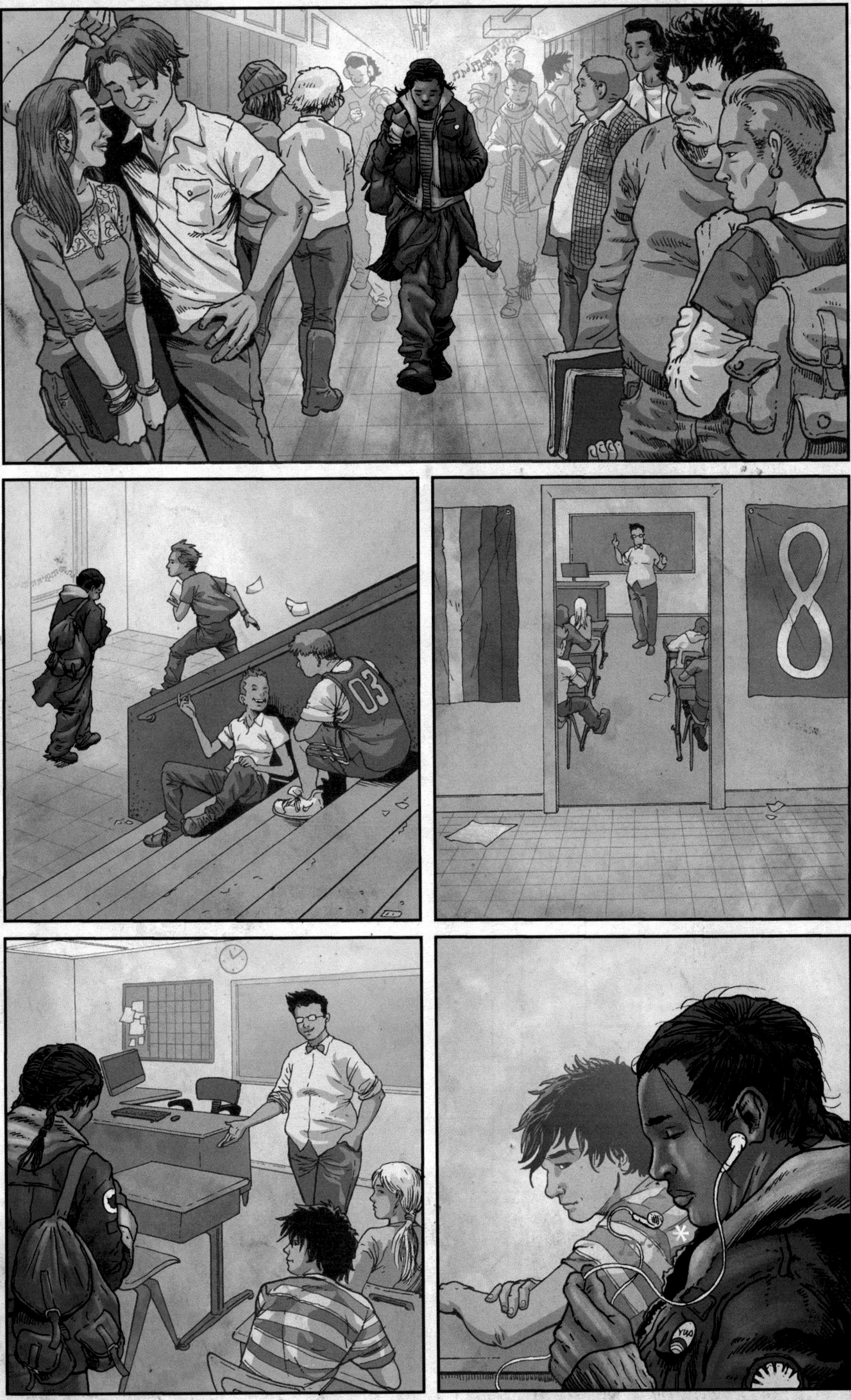

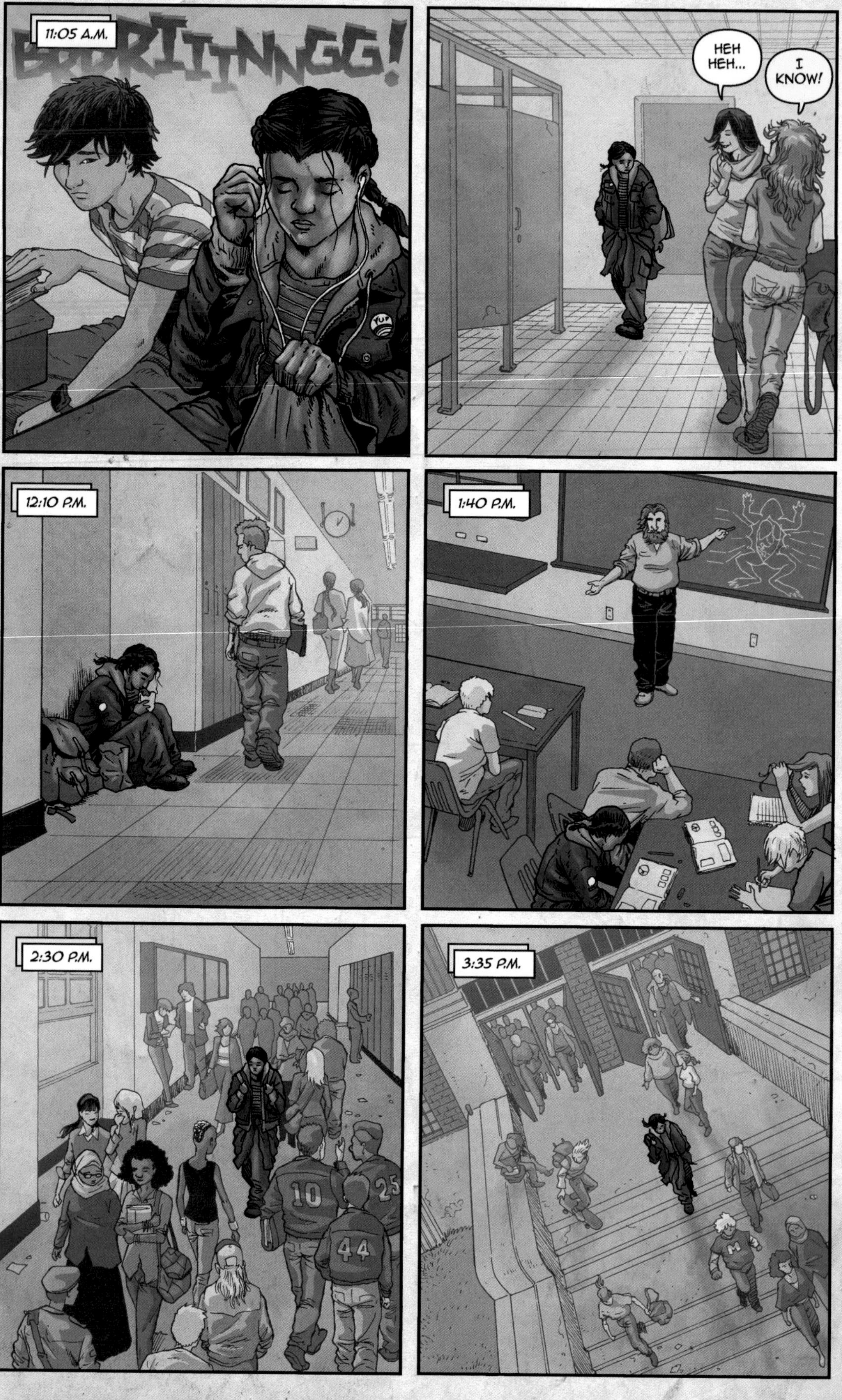
11:05 A.M.
BRRIIINNGG!
HEH HEH...
I KNOW!
12:10 P.M.
1:40 P.M.
2:30 P.M.
3:35 P.M.

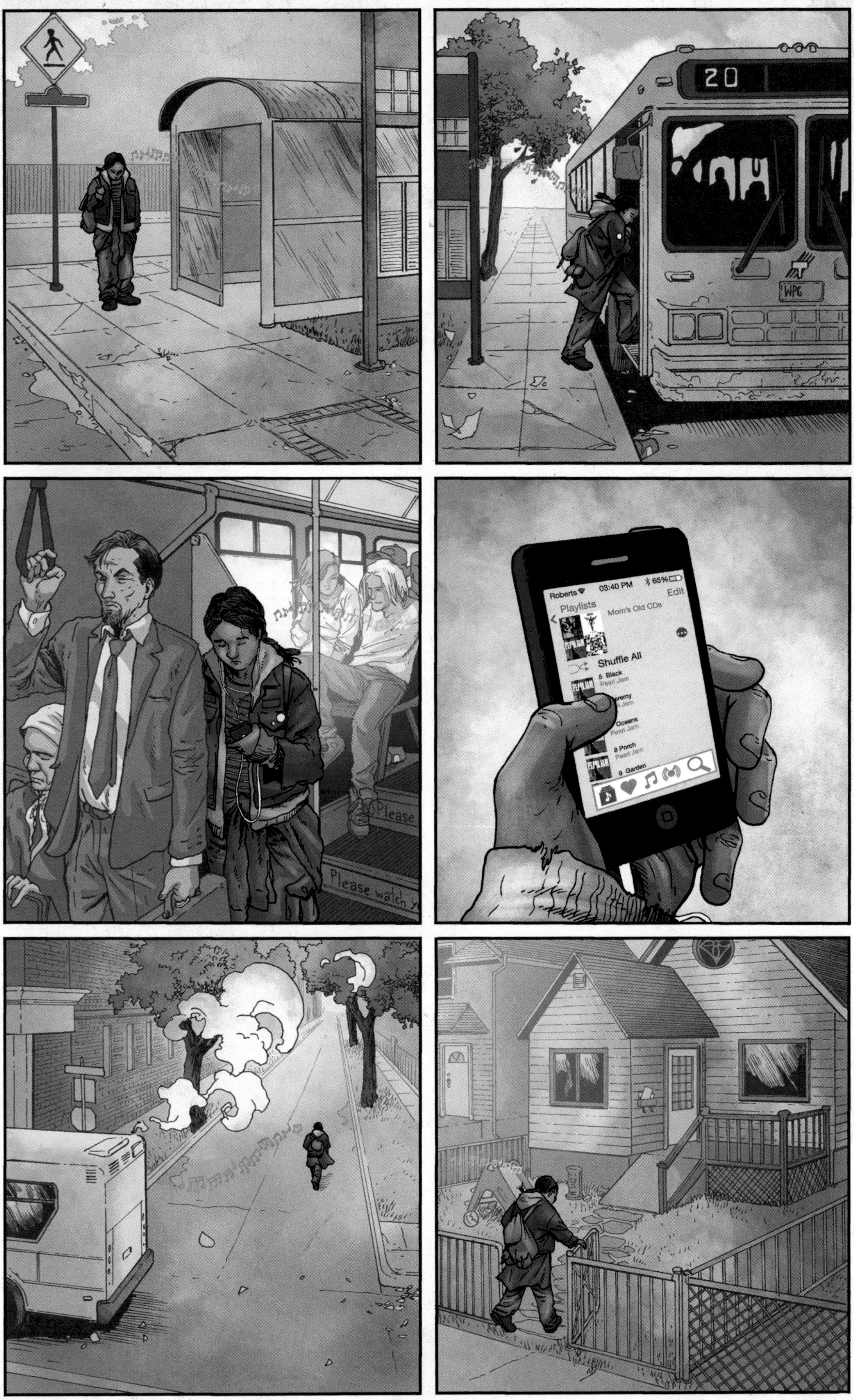
20
WPG
Please
Roberts
03:40 PM
65%
Edit
Playlists
Mom's Old CDs
Shuffle All
5 Black
Pearl Jam
8 Porch
Pearl Jam
9 Garden

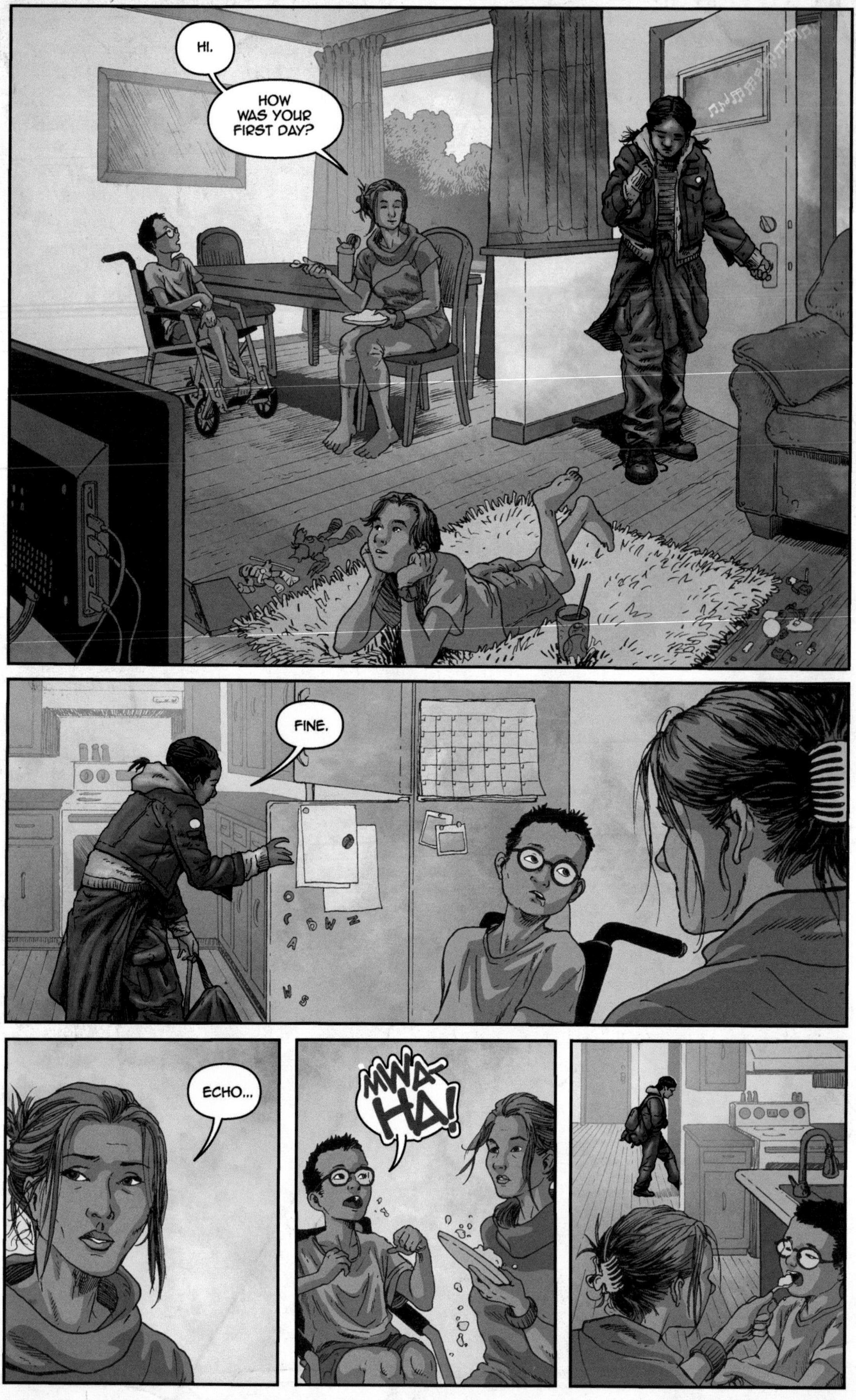
HI.
HOW WAS YOUR FIRST DAY?
FINE.
ECHO...
MWA-HA!

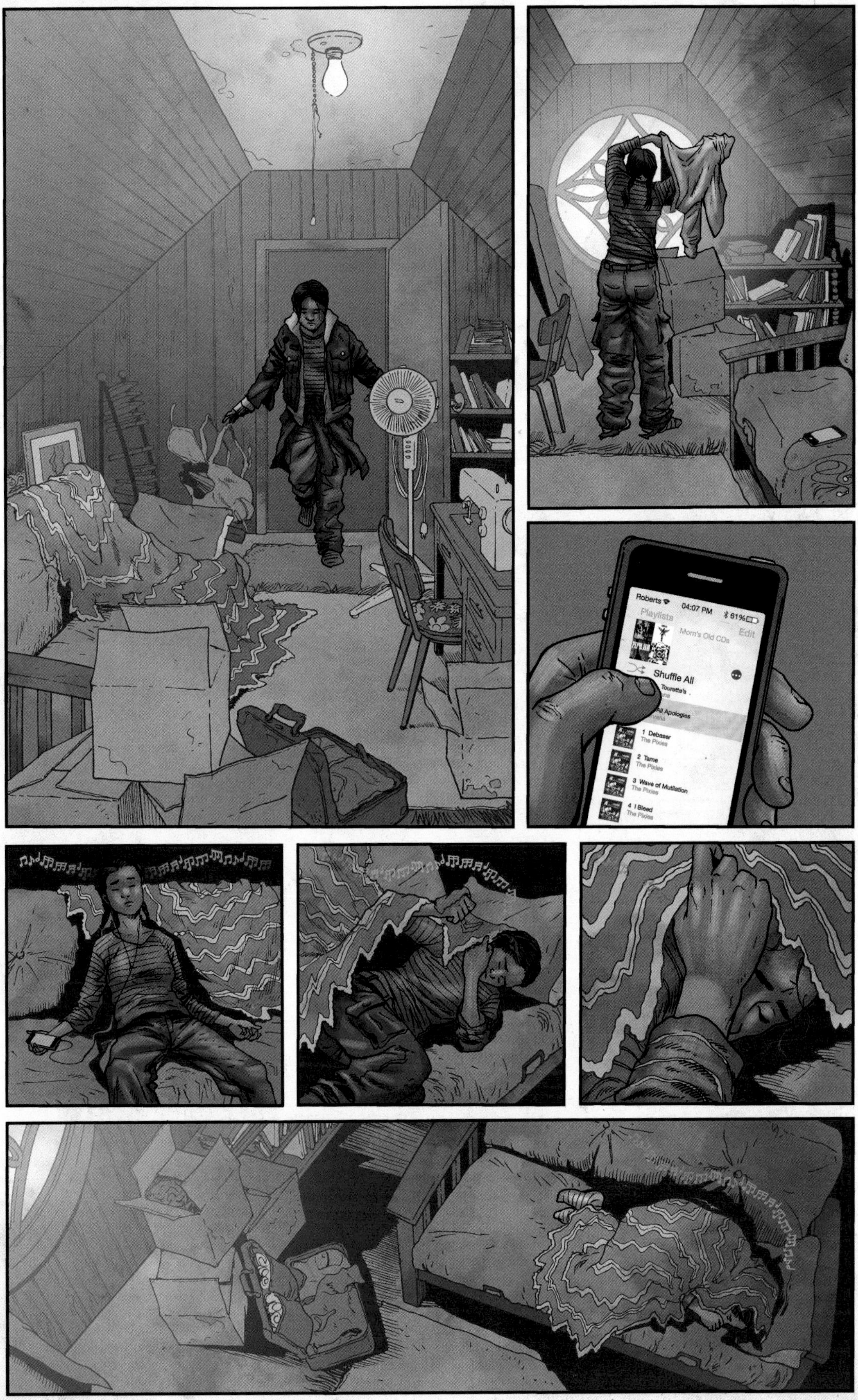
Roberts
04:07 PM
61%
Playlists
Mom's Old CDs
Edit
Shuffle All
Tourette's
All Apologies
1 Debaser
The Pixies
2 Tame
The Pixies
3 Wave of Mutilation
The Pixies
4 I Bleed
The Pixies

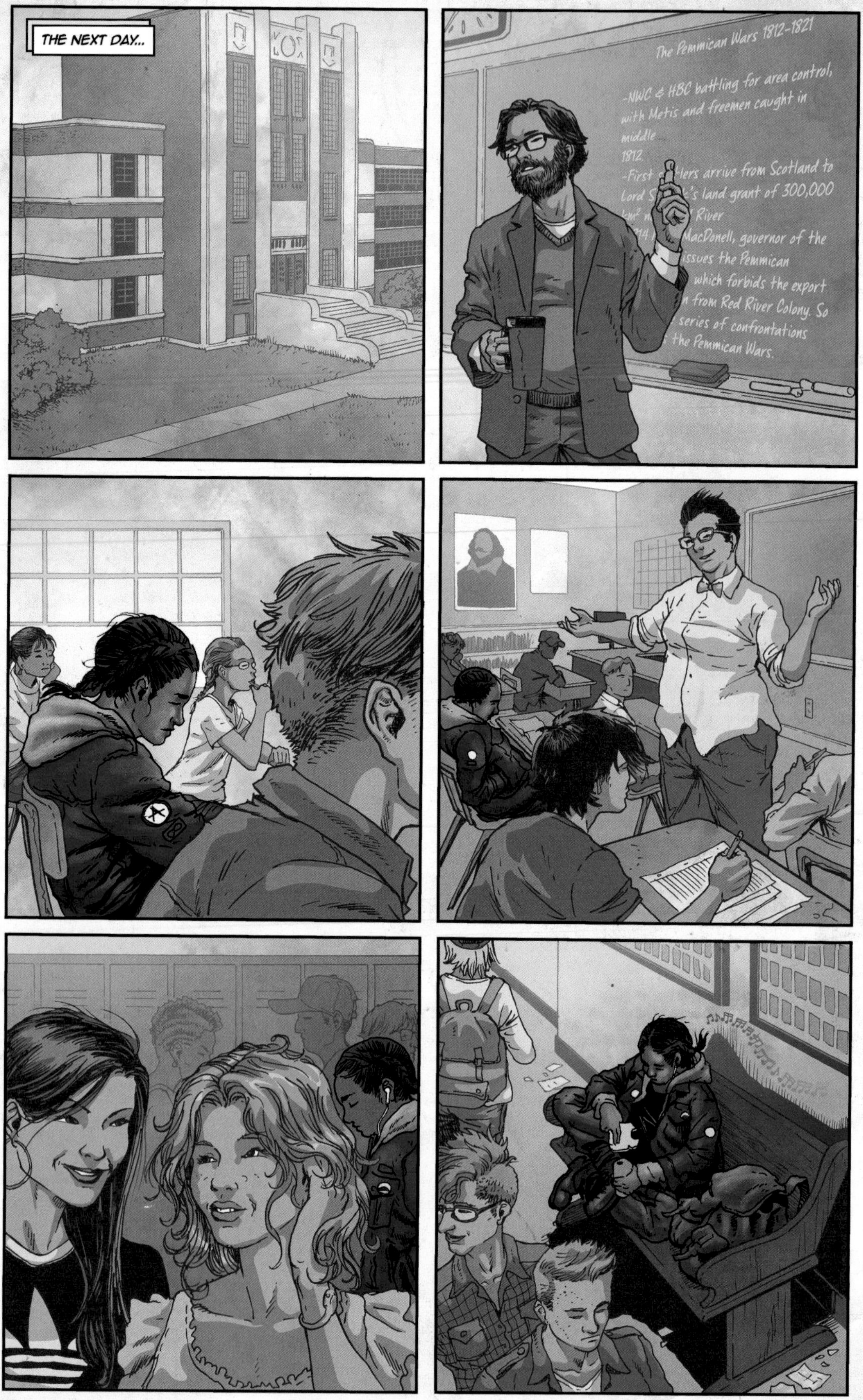
THE NEXT DAY...
The Pemmican Wars 1812-1821
-NWC & HBC battling for area control, with Metis and freemen caught in middle
1812.
-First
tlers arrive from Scotland to
Lord S
's land grant of 300,000
River
MacDonell, governor of the
issues the Pemmican
which forbids the export
from Red River Colony. So
series of confrontations
the Pemmican Wars.

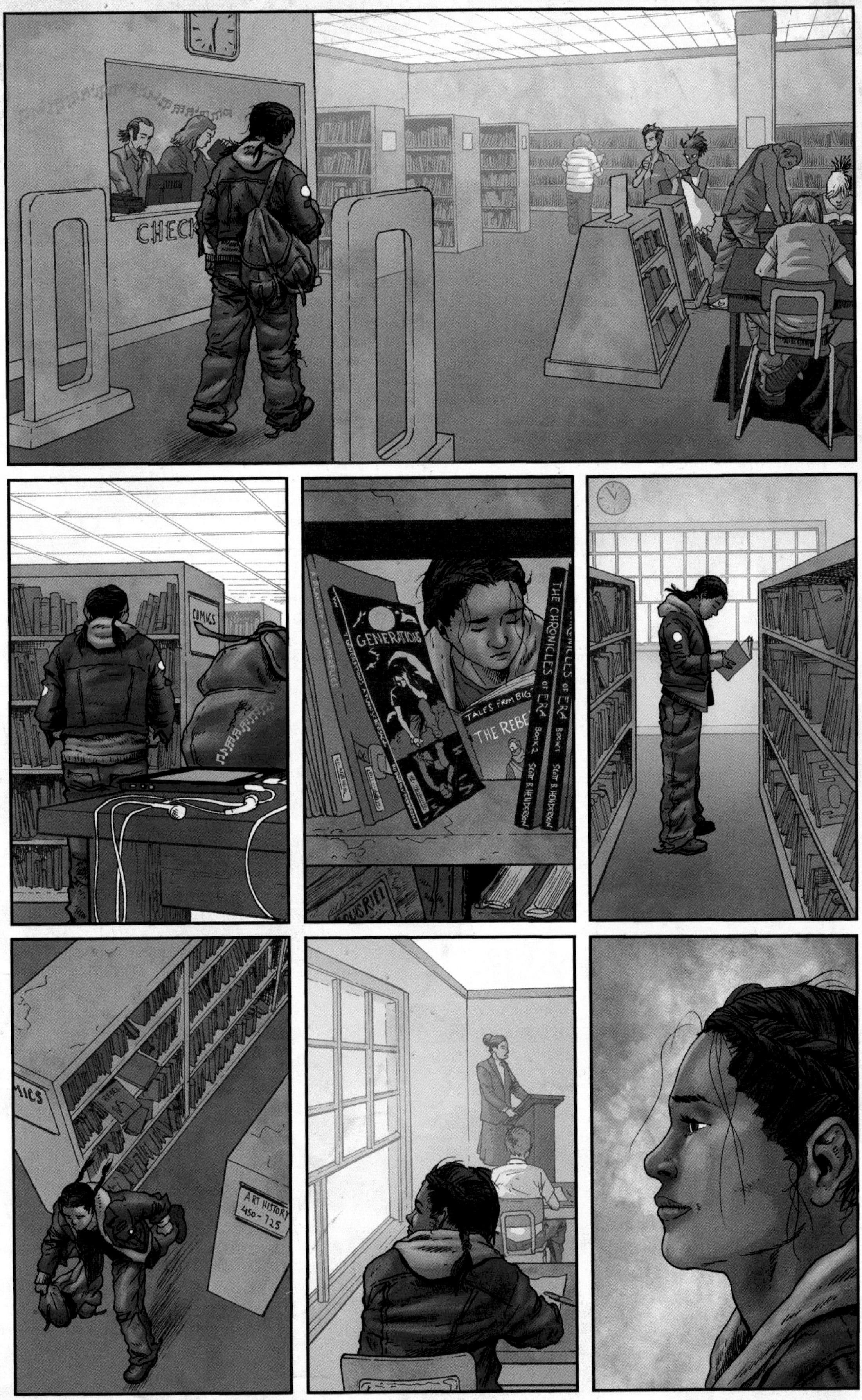
CHECK
COMICS
GENERATIONS
TALES FROM BIG
THE REBE
THE CHRONICLES OF ERA
BOOK 2
SCOTT B. HENDERSON
MICS
ART HISTORY
450-725

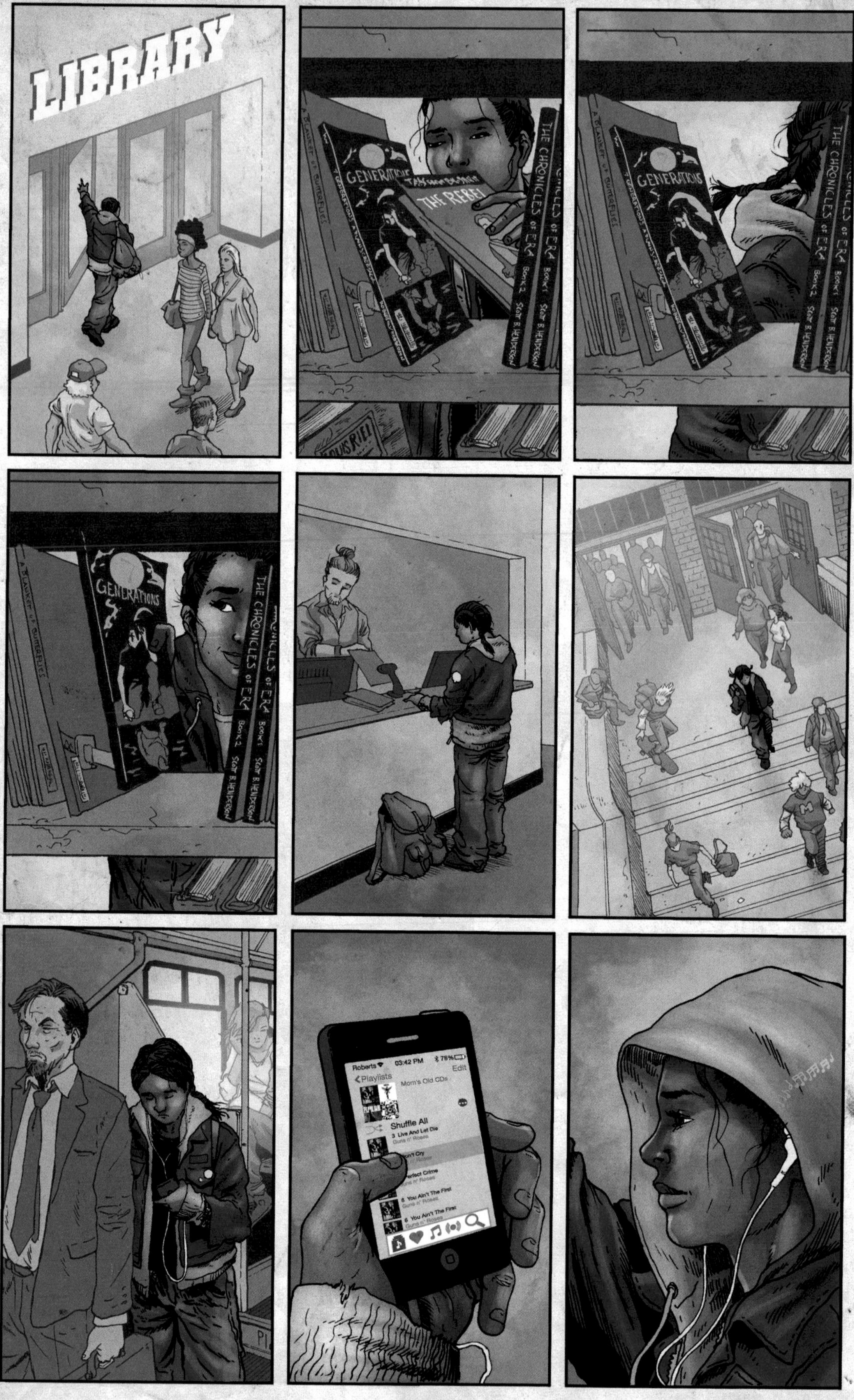

LIBRARY
GENERATIONS
THE REBEL
THE CHRONICLES of ERA
BOOK 1
BOOK 2
SCOTT B. HENDERSON
A BLANKET of BUTTERFLIES
Roberts
03:42 PM
78%
Edit
Playlists
Mom's Old CDs
Shuffle All
3 Live And Let Die
Guns n' Roses
6 You Ain't The First
Guns n' Roses
6 You Ain't The First
Guns n' Roses

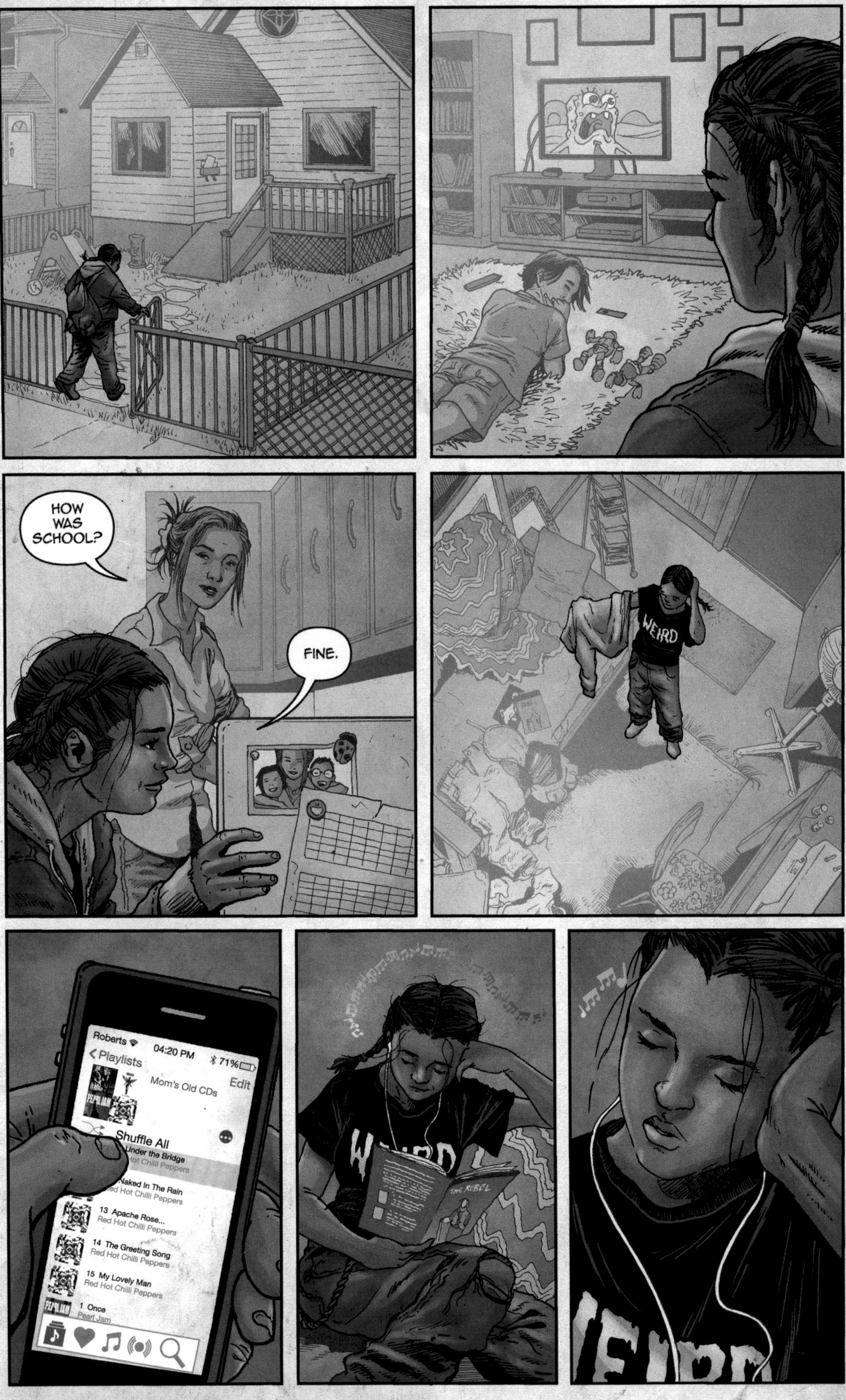
HOW WAS SCHOOL?
FINE.
WEIRD
Roberts
04:20 PM
71%
Playlists
Mom's Old CDs
Edit
Shuffle All
Under the Bridge
Naked In The Rain
13 Apache Rose...
Red Hot Chilli Peppers
14 The Greeting Song
Red Hot Chilli Peppers
15 My Lovely Man
Red Hot Chilli Peppers
1 Once
Pearl Jam
THE REBEL

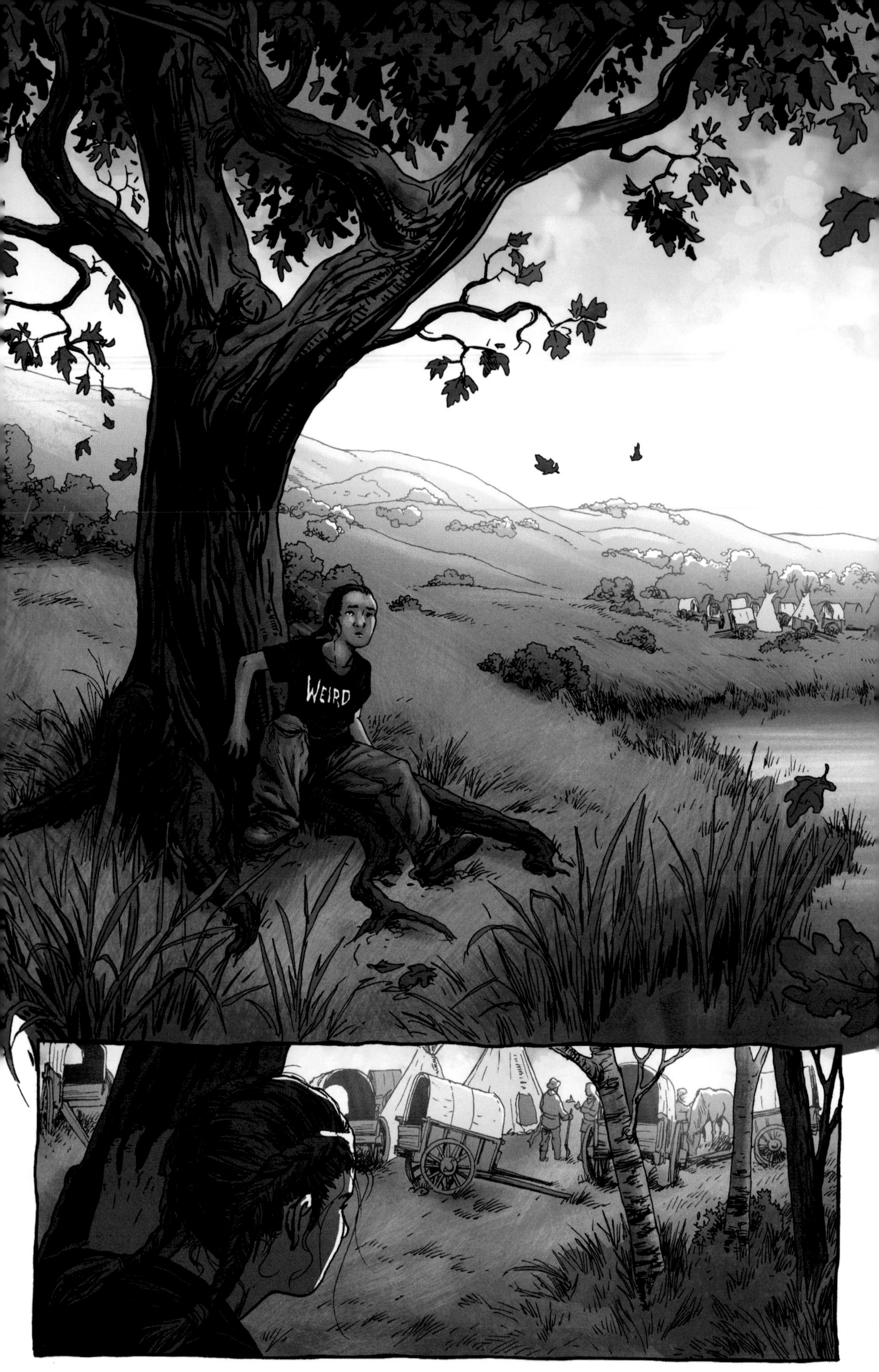
WEIRD

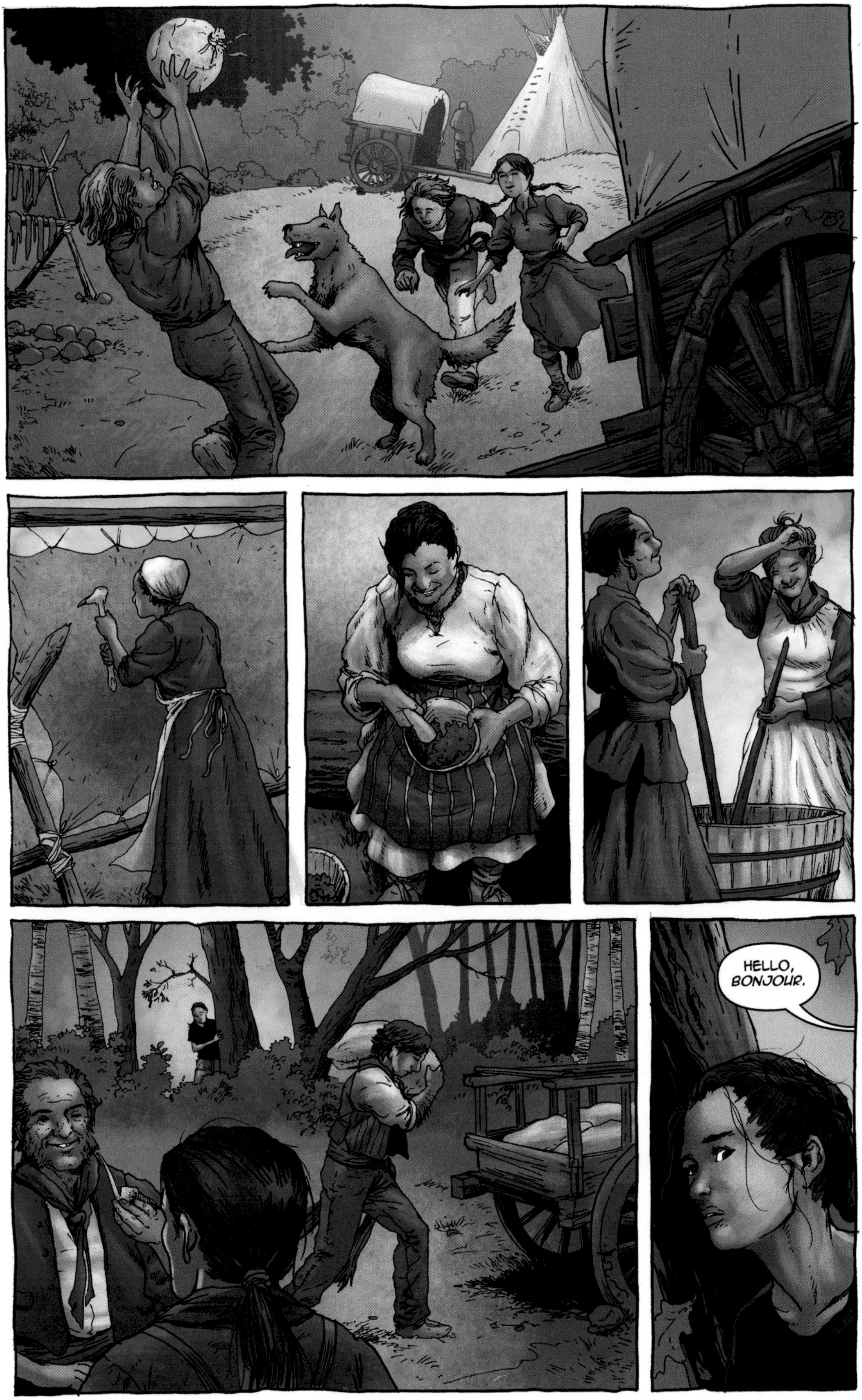
HELLO, BONJOUR.

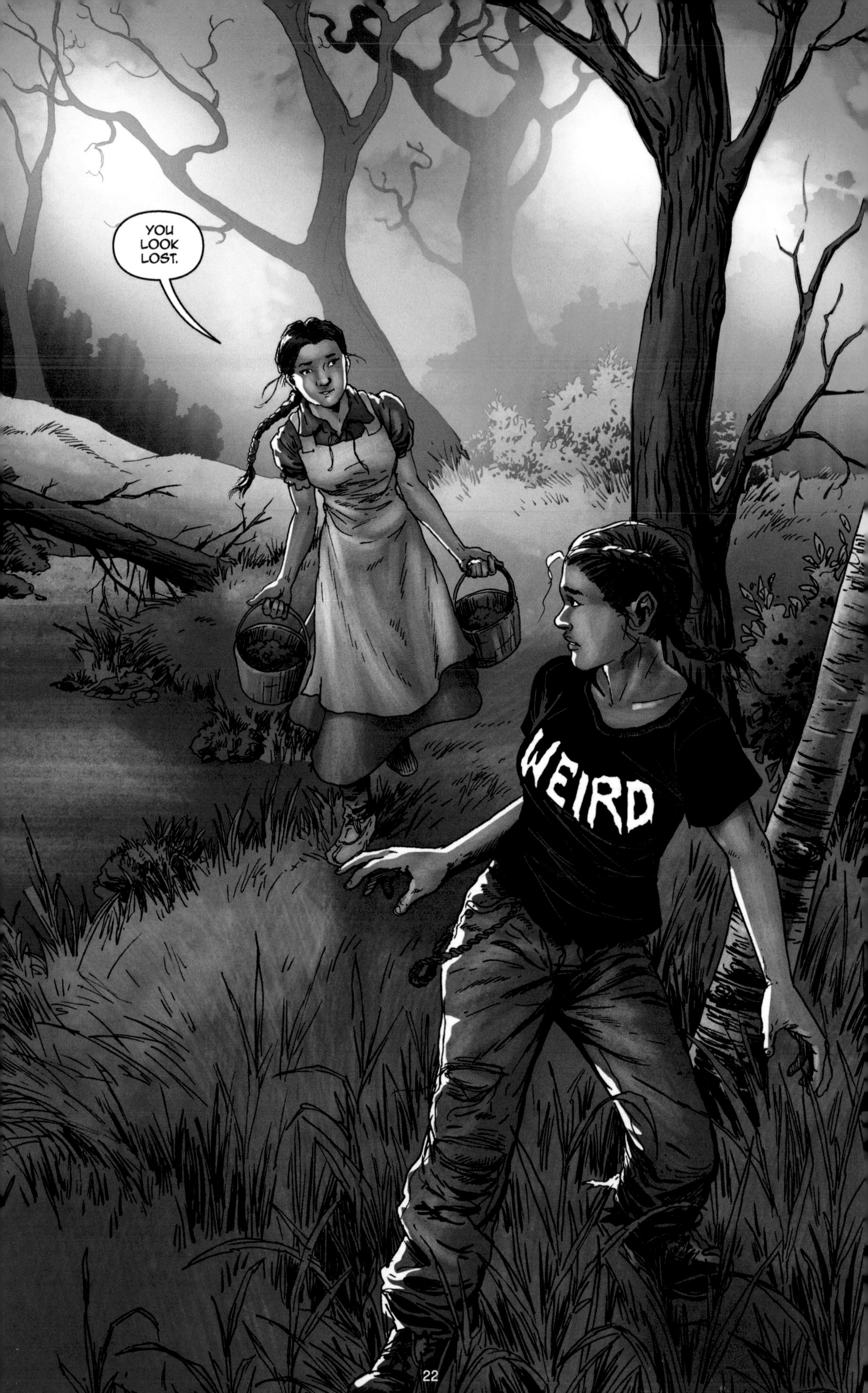
YOU LOOK LOST.
WEIRD

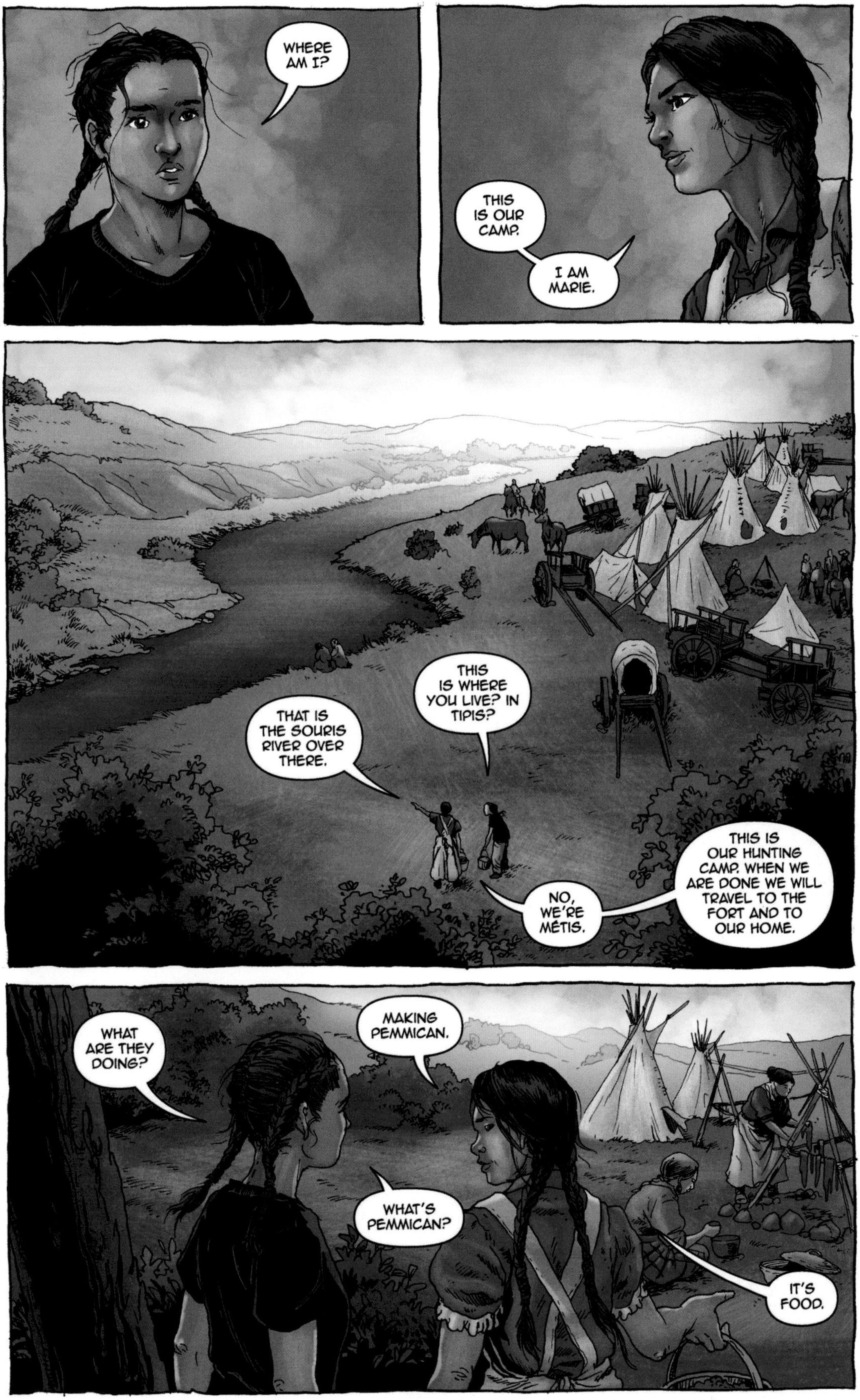
WHERE AM I?
THIS IS OUR CAMP.
I AM MARIE.
THAT IS THE SOURIS RIVER OVER THERE.
THIS IS WHERE YOU LIVE? IN TIPIS?
NO, WE'RE MÉTIS.
THIS IS OUR HUNTING CAMP. WHEN WE ARE DONE WE WILL TRAVEL TO THE FORT AND TO OUR HOME.
WHAT ARE THEY DOING?
MAKING PEMMICAN.
WHAT'S PEMMICAN?
IT'S FOOD.

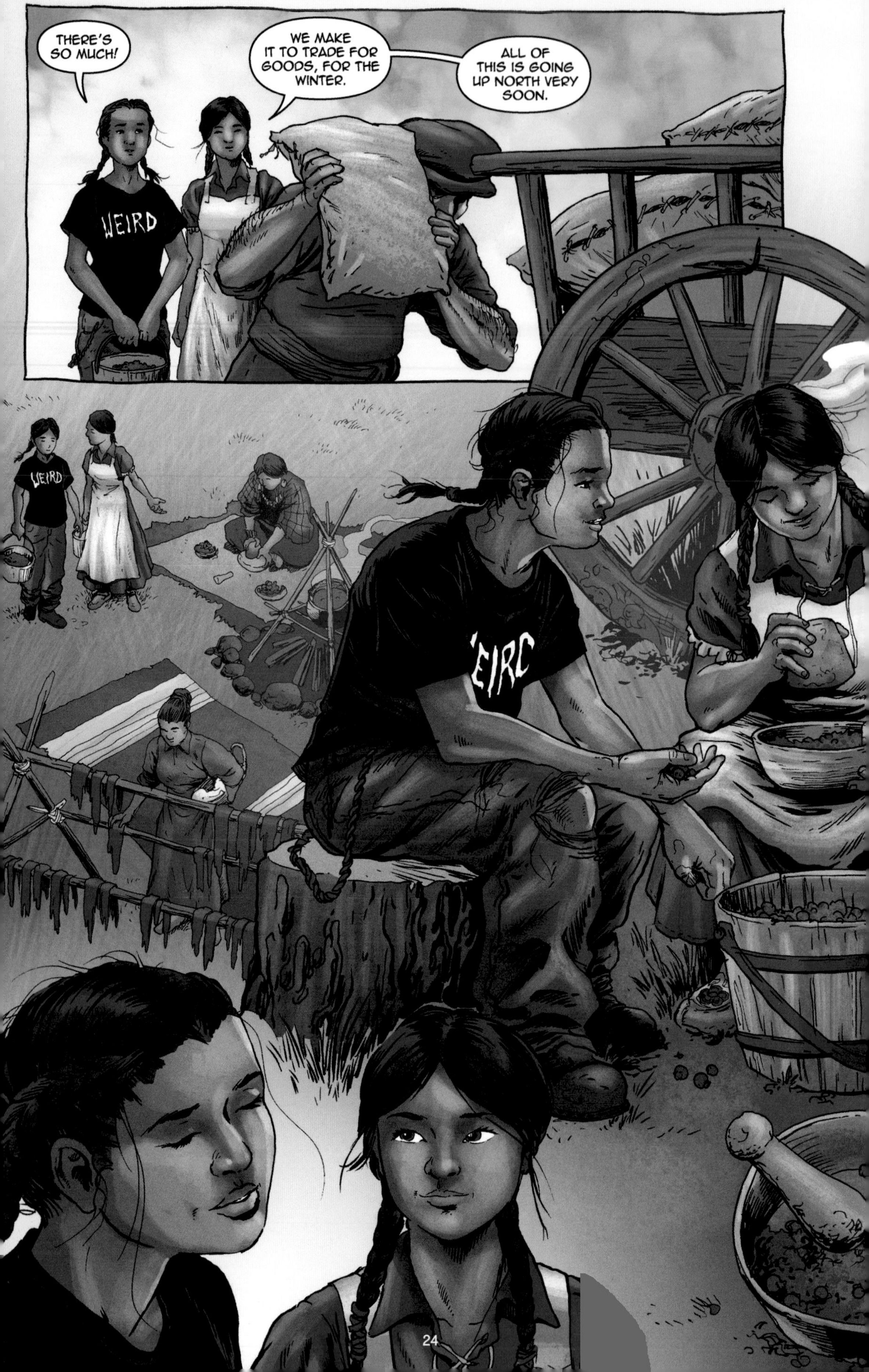

THERE'S SO MUCH!
WE MAKE IT TO TRADE FOR GOODS, FOR THE WINTER.
ALL OF THIS IS GOING UP NORTH VERY SOON.
WEIRD

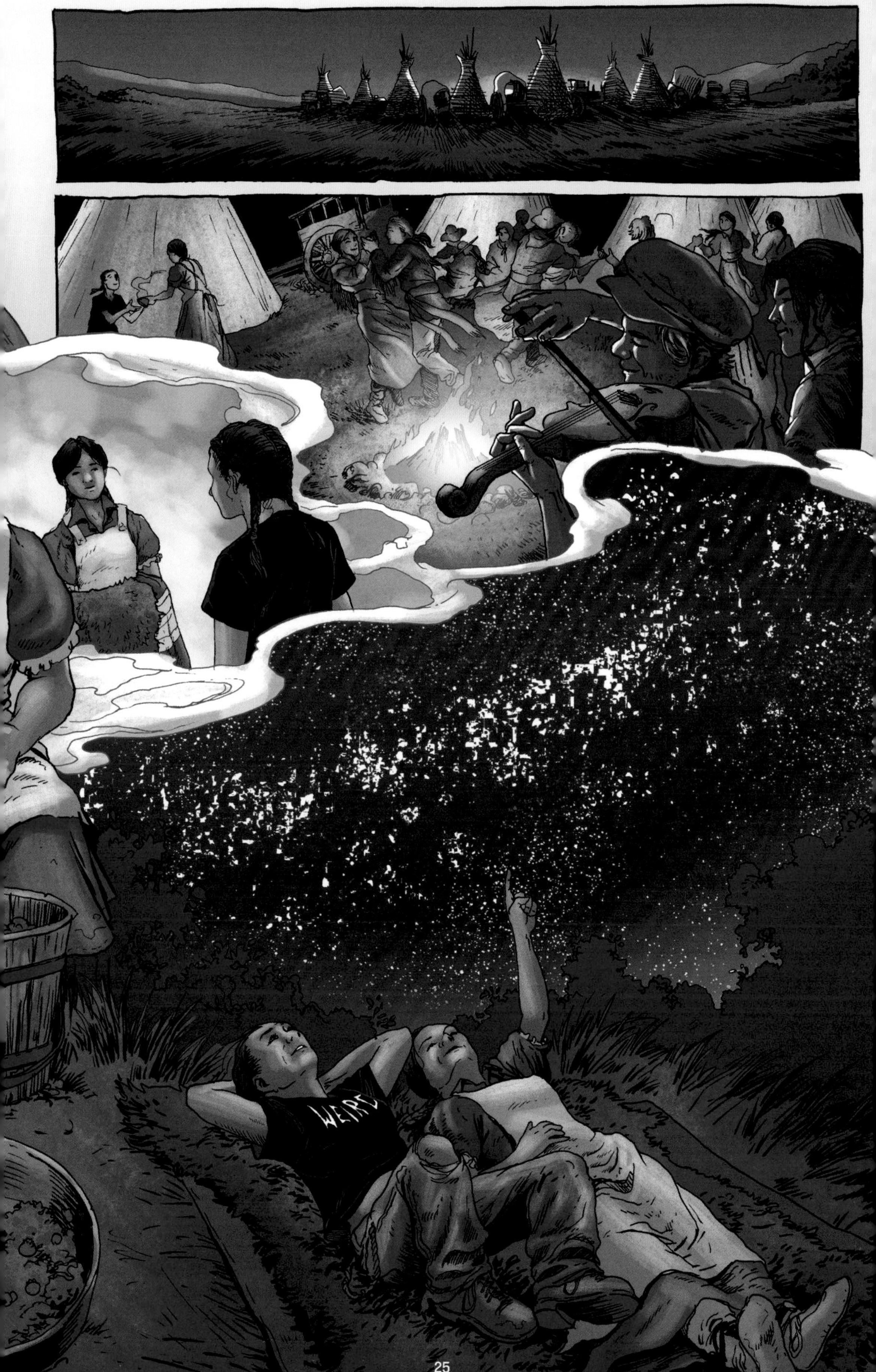
WEIRD

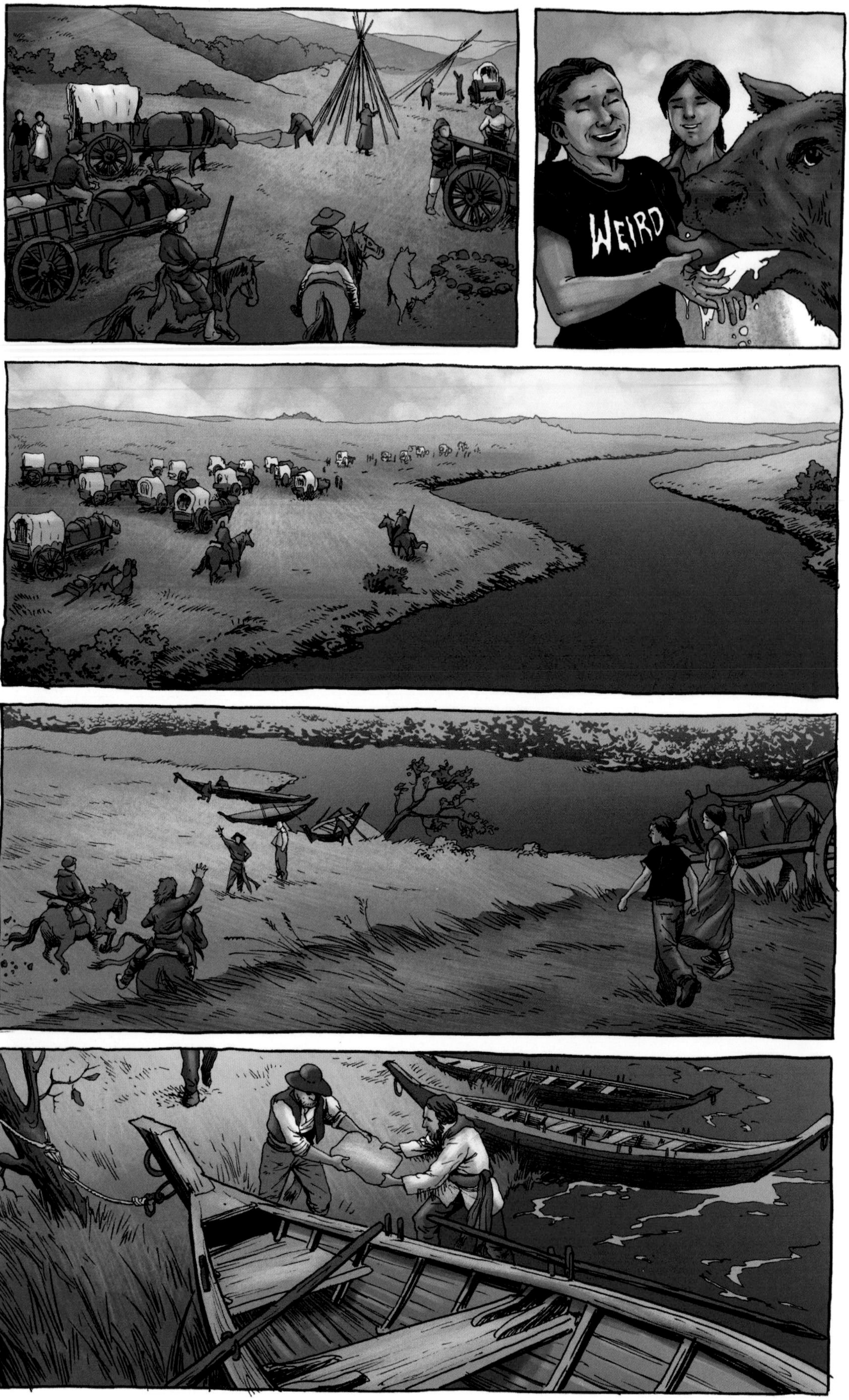
WEIRD

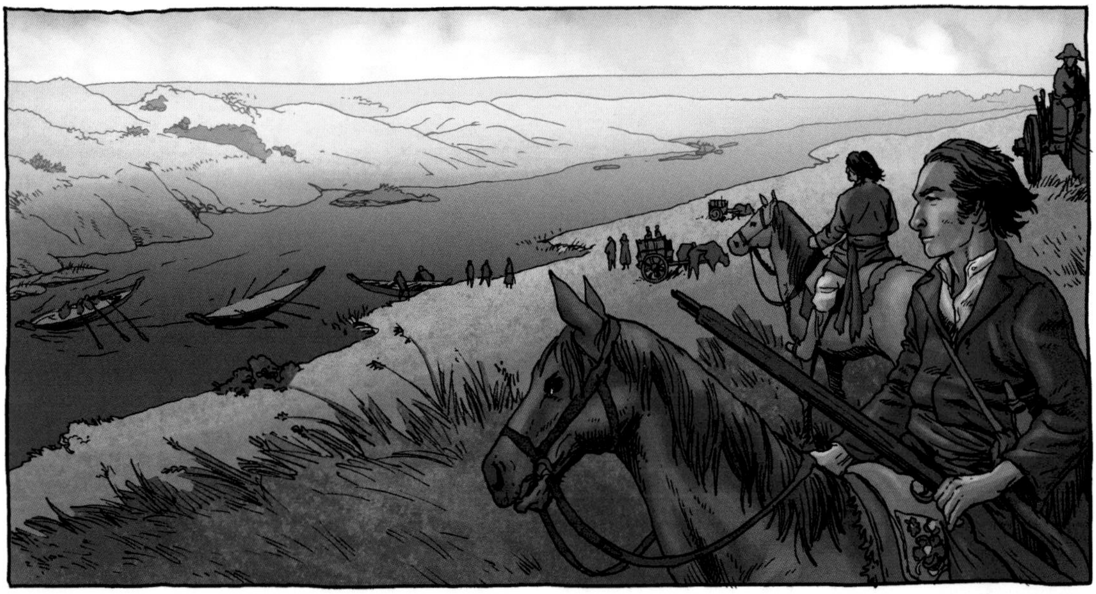

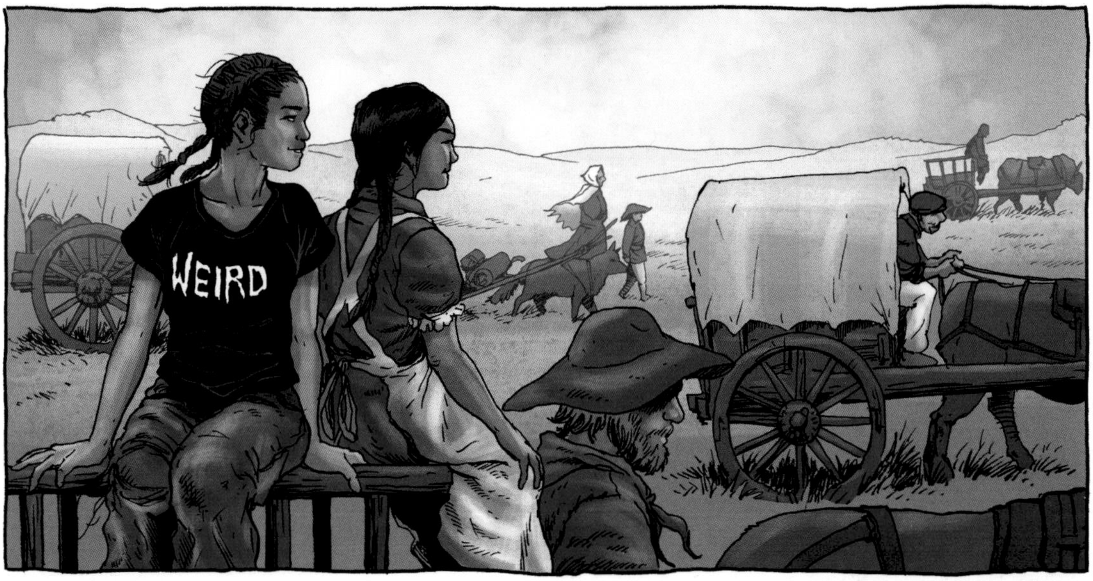
WEIRD

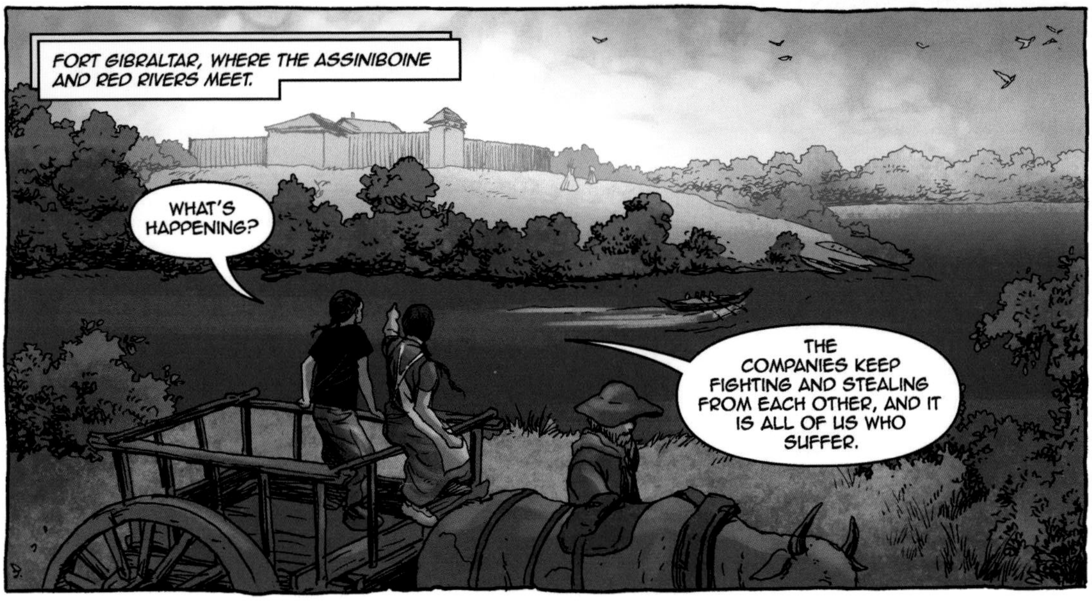
FORT GIBRALTAR, WHERE THE ASSINIBOINE AND RED RIVERS MEET.
WHAT'S HAPPENING?
THE COMPANIES KEEP FIGHTING AND STEALING FROM EACH OTHER, AND IT IS ALL OF US WHO SUFFER.

MES AMIS, THE GOVERNOR HAS PASSED ANOTHER *PROCLAMATION.*

WHAT? WHAT IS THIS?

WHAT HAS HE DONE NOW?

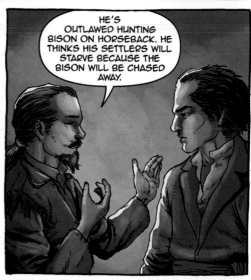

HE'S OUTLAWED HUNTING BISON ON HORSEBACK. HE THINKS HIS SETTLERS WILL STARVE BECAUSE THE BISON WILL BE CHASED AWAY.

WE WILL *ALL* STARVE IF WE ARE NOT ALLOWED TO HUNT.

THERE IS NOTHING MORE WE CAN DO.

YES THERE IS.

WE CAN FIGHT BACK.

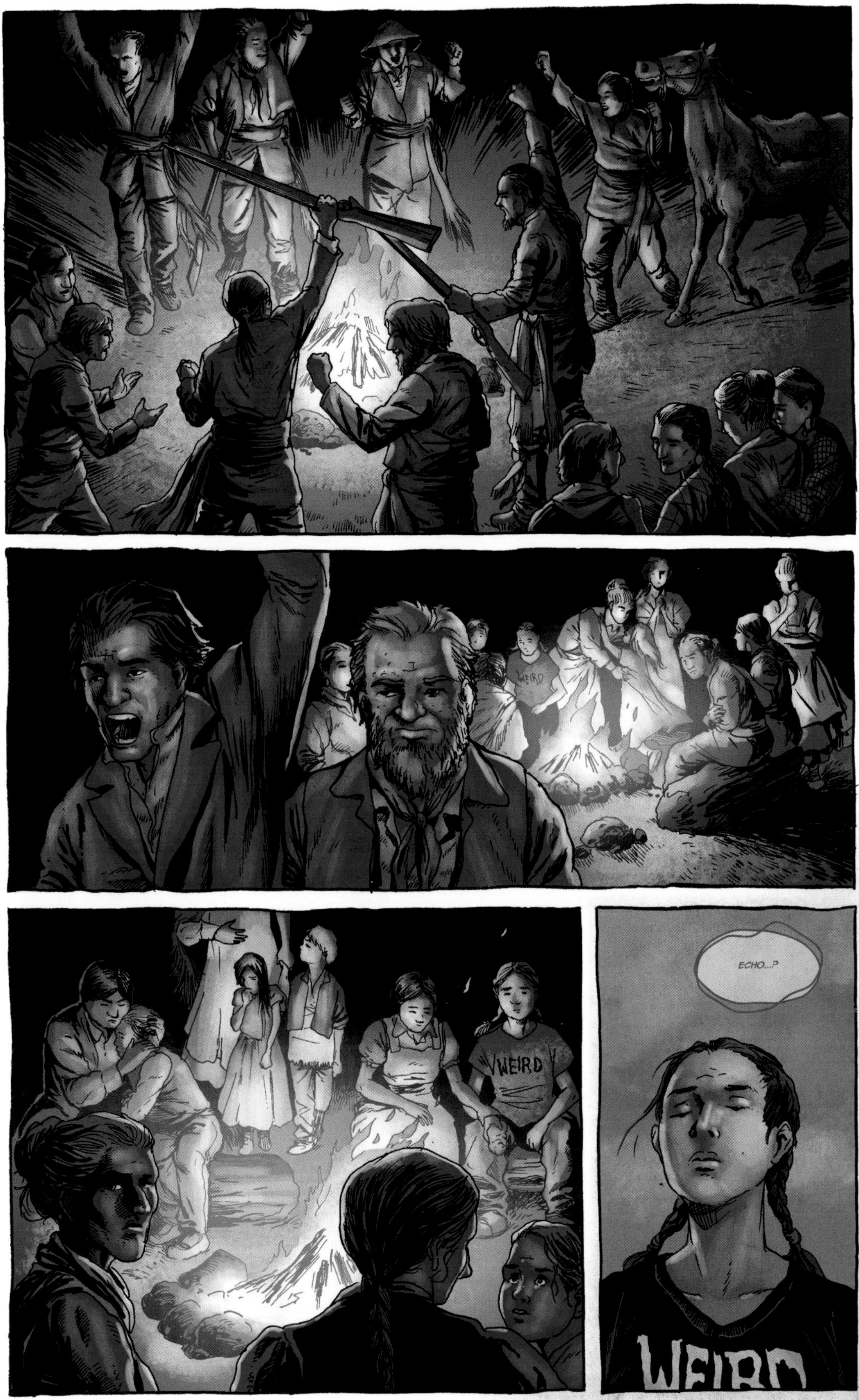
ECHO...?
WEIRD

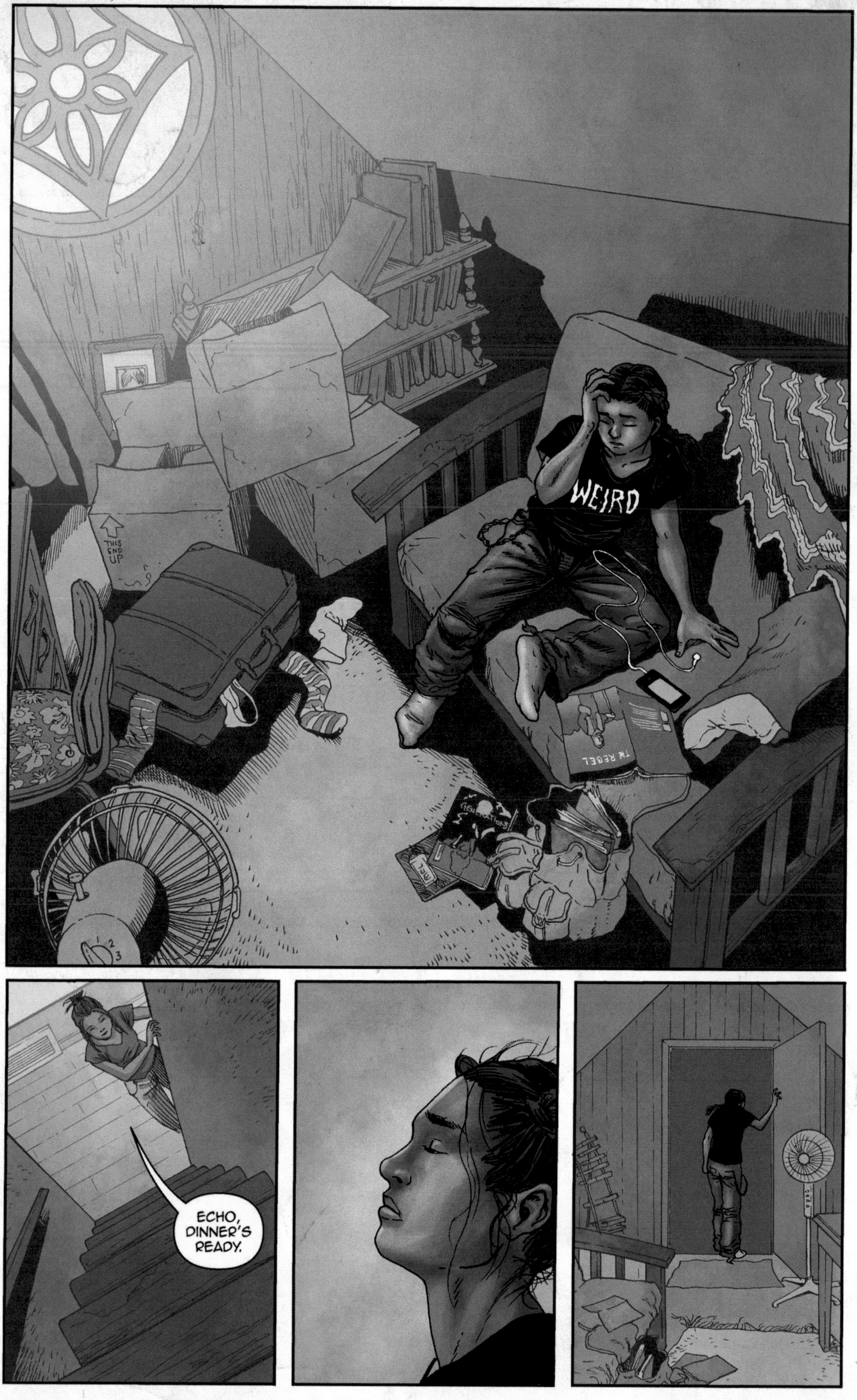
WEIRD
THIS END UP
THE REBEL
ECHO, DINNER'S READY.

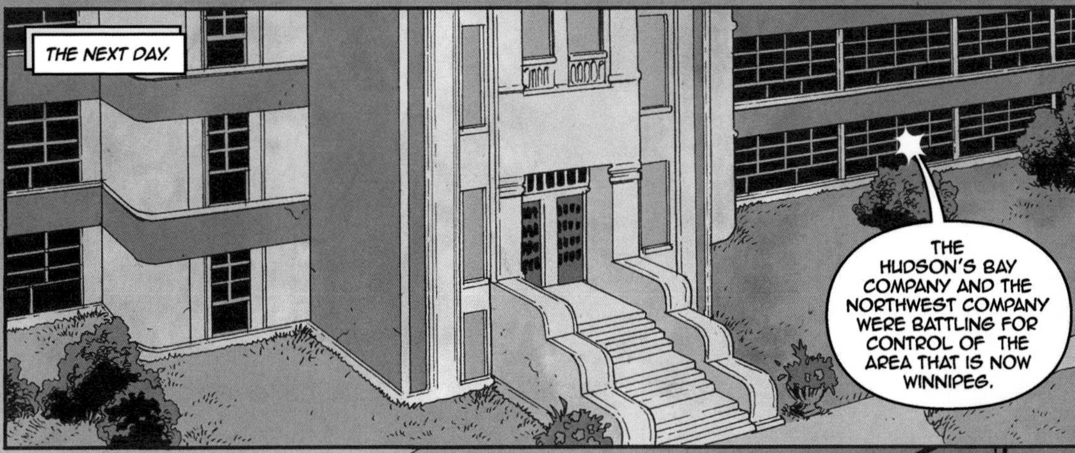
THE NEXT DAY.
THE HUDSON'S BAY COMPANY AND THE NORTHWEST COMPANY WERE BATTLING FOR CONTROL OF THE AREA THAT IS NOW WINNIPEG.

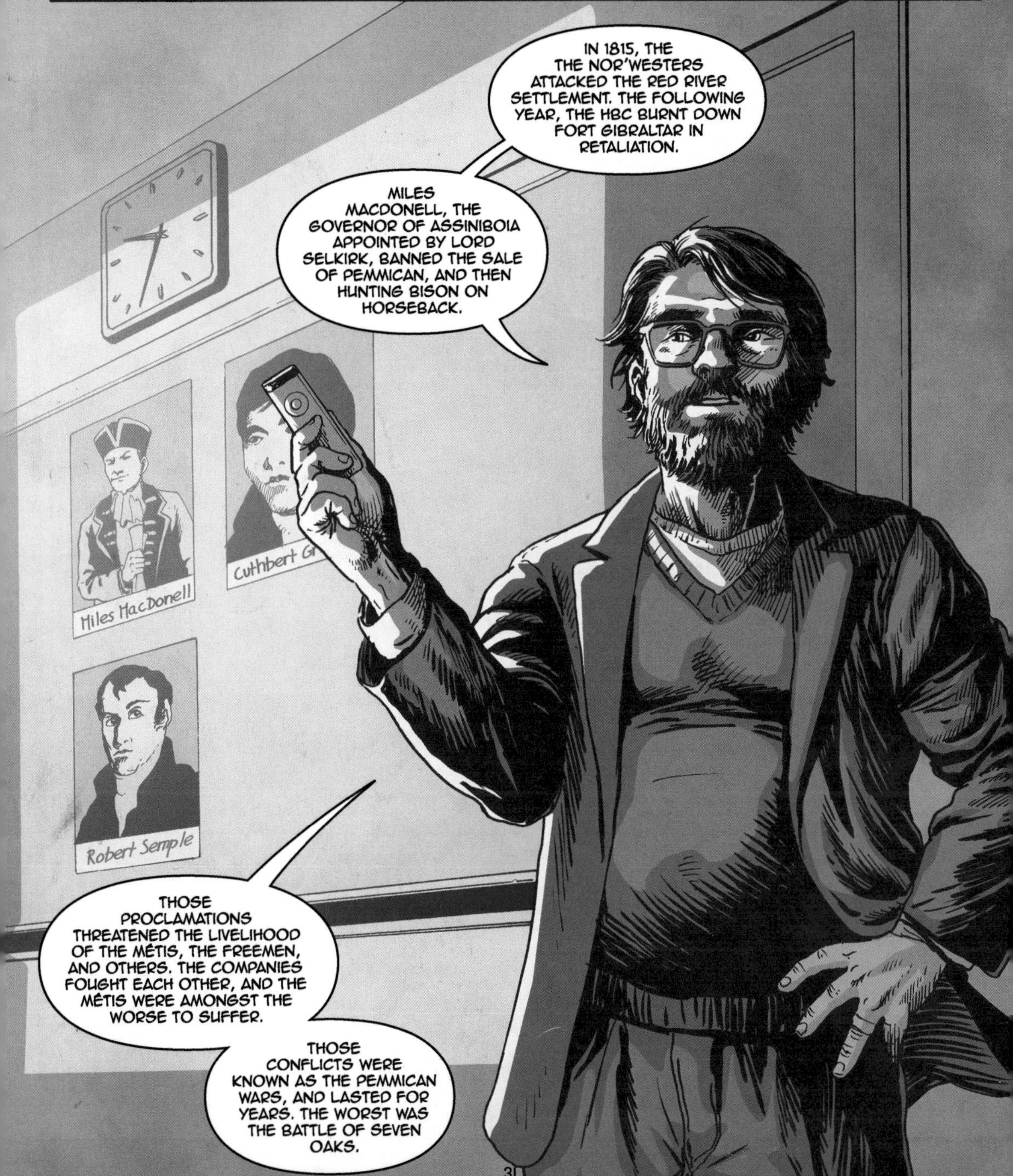
IN 1815, THE THE NOR'WESTERS ATTACKED THE RED RIVER SETTLEMENT. THE FOLLOWING YEAR, THE HBC BURNT DOWN FORT GIBRALTAR IN RETALIATION.
MILES MACDONELL, THE GOVERNOR OF ASSINIBOIA APPOINTED BY LORD SELKIRK, BANNED THE SALE OF PEMMICAN, AND THEN HUNTING BISON ON HORSEBACK.
Miles MacDonell
Cuthbert Gr
Robert Semple
THOSE PROCLAMATIONS THREATENED THE LIVELIHOOD OF THE MÉTIS, THE FREEMEN, AND OTHERS. THE COMPANIES FOUGHT EACH OTHER, AND THE MÉTIS WERE AMONGST THE WORSE TO SUFFER.
THOSE CONFLICTS WERE KNOWN AS THE PEMMICAN WARS, AND LASTED FOR YEARS. THE WORST WAS THE BATTLE OF SEVEN OAKS.

On June 19, 1816, Cuthbert Grant was going east with more than 60 men on horseback to trade pemmican with members of the Northwest Company. Governor Semple and 28 Hudson Bay's Company men stopped them at the place called the Grenouillère (Frog Plain) or Seven Oaks.

Figure 9.13 At the Battle of Seven Oaks, Métis supporters of the Northwest Company fought with the settlers of Red River.

Rise of the Métis

...growing between the Hudson's Bay Company ...Company. The Hudson's Bay Company ...ting the land around the Red and ...st Company wanted to keep ...ng of 1816, the...

After a... out between... settlers and the... The Métis were the...

In 1815, he was appo... of the Hudson's Ba... territories by Lo...

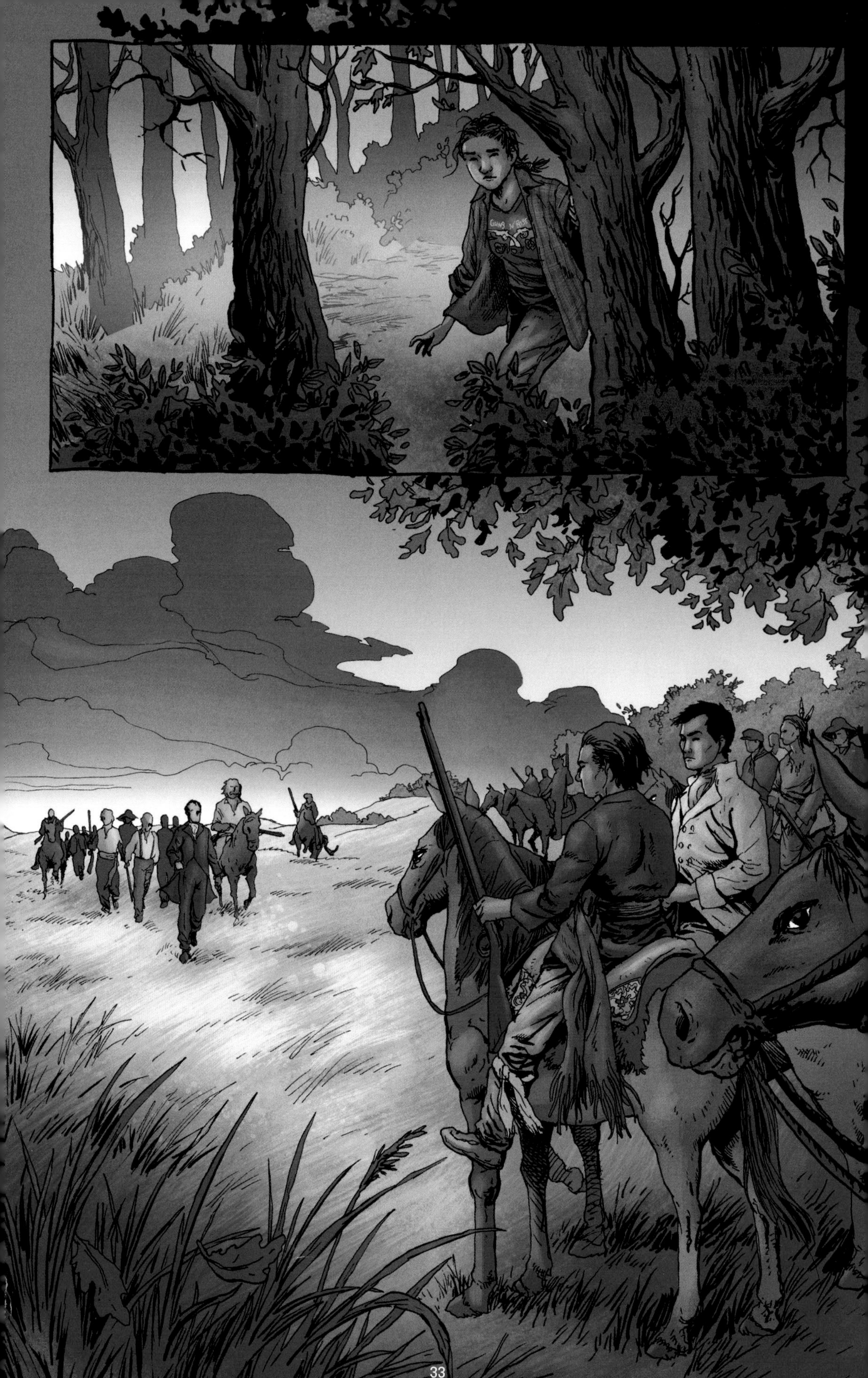

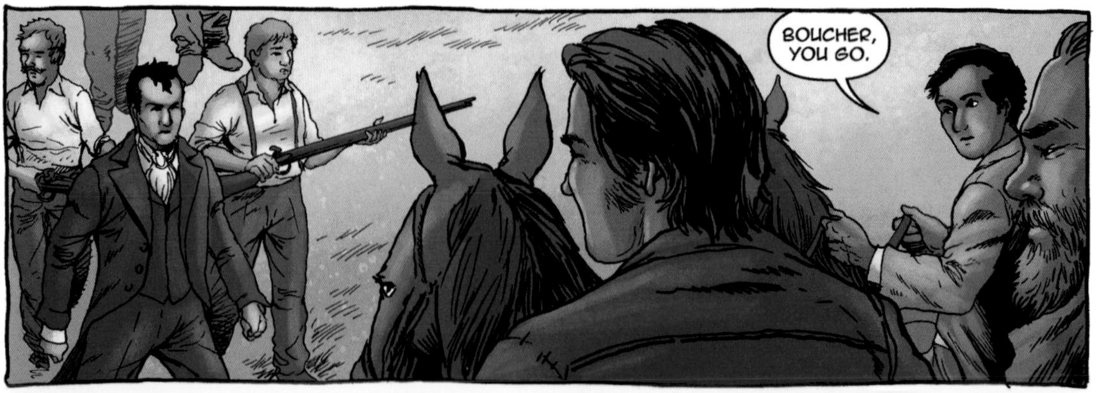
BOUCHER, YOU GO.

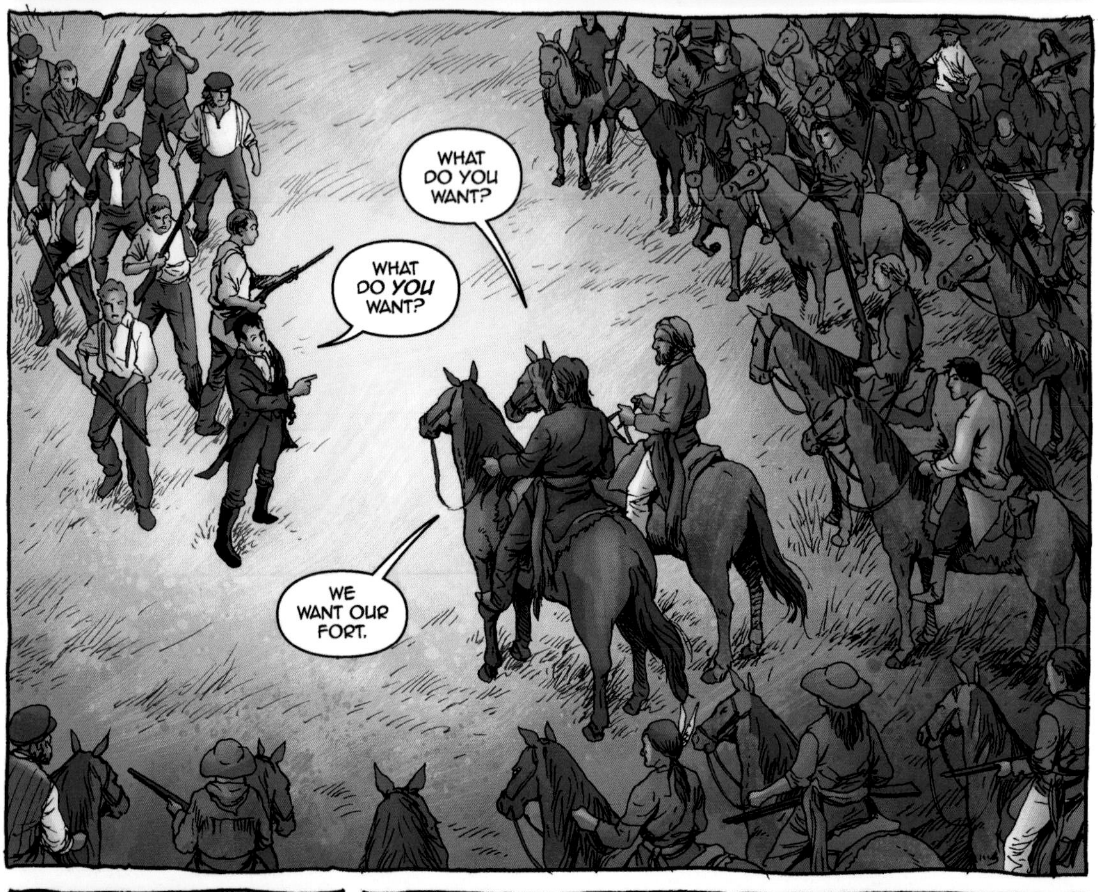
WHAT DO YOU WANT?
WHAT DO *YOU* WANT?
WE WANT OUR FORT.

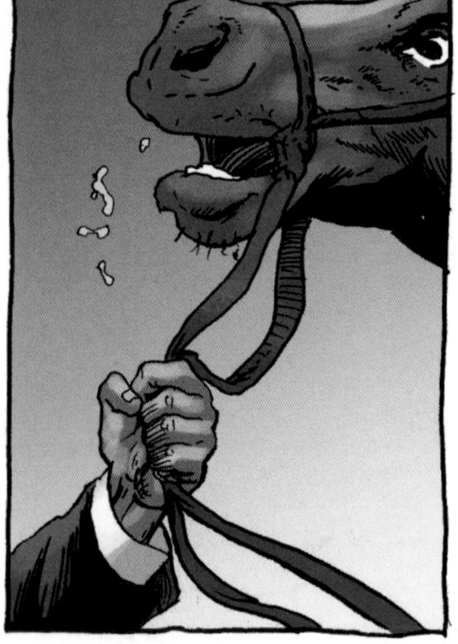

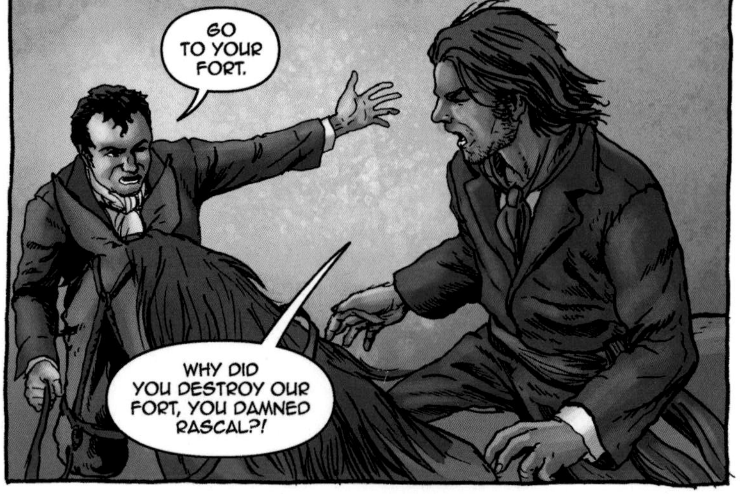
GO TO YOUR FORT.
WHY DID YOU DESTROY OUR FORT, YOU DAMNED RASCAL?!

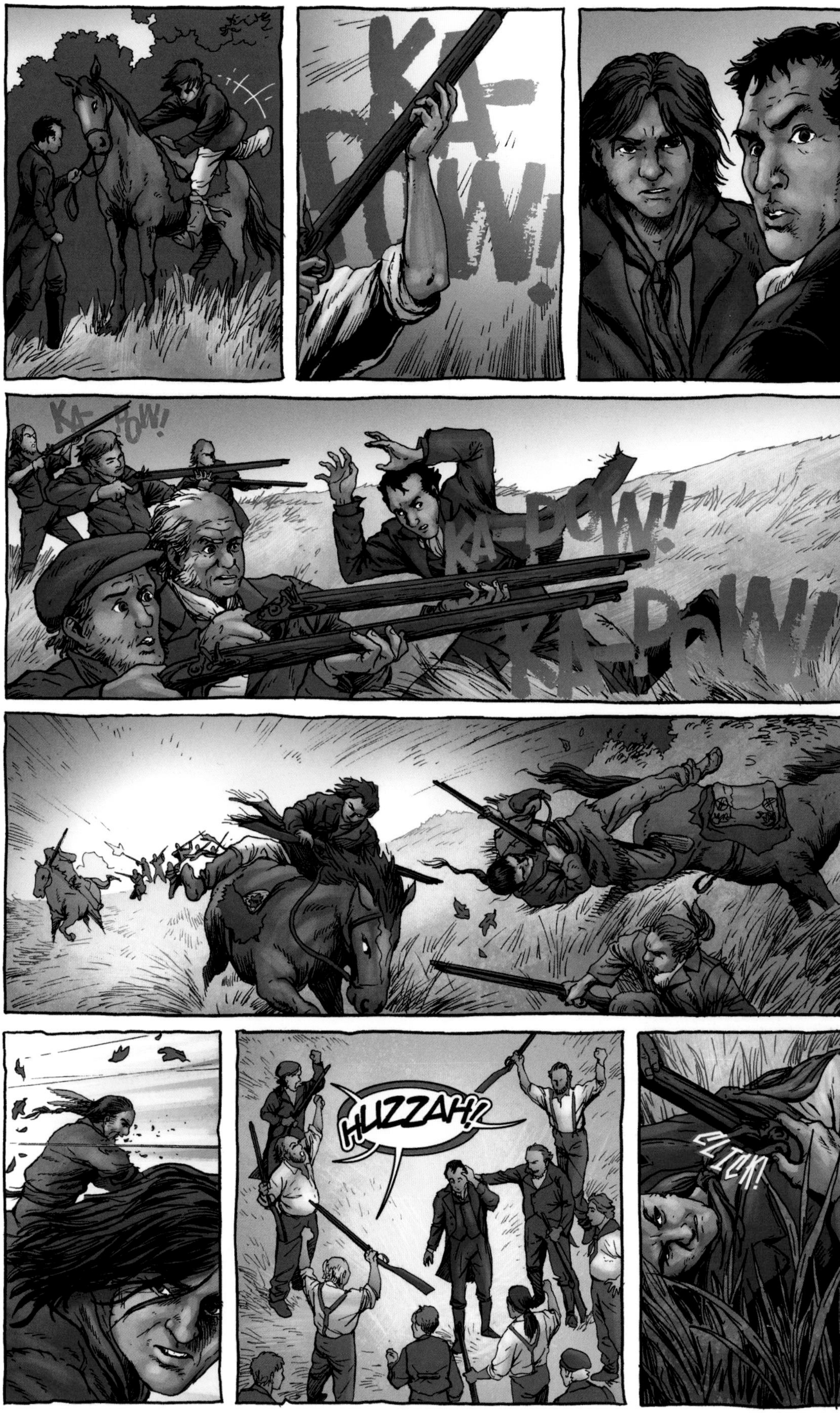
KA-POW!
KA-POW!
KA-POW!
KA-POW!
HUZZAH!
CLICK!

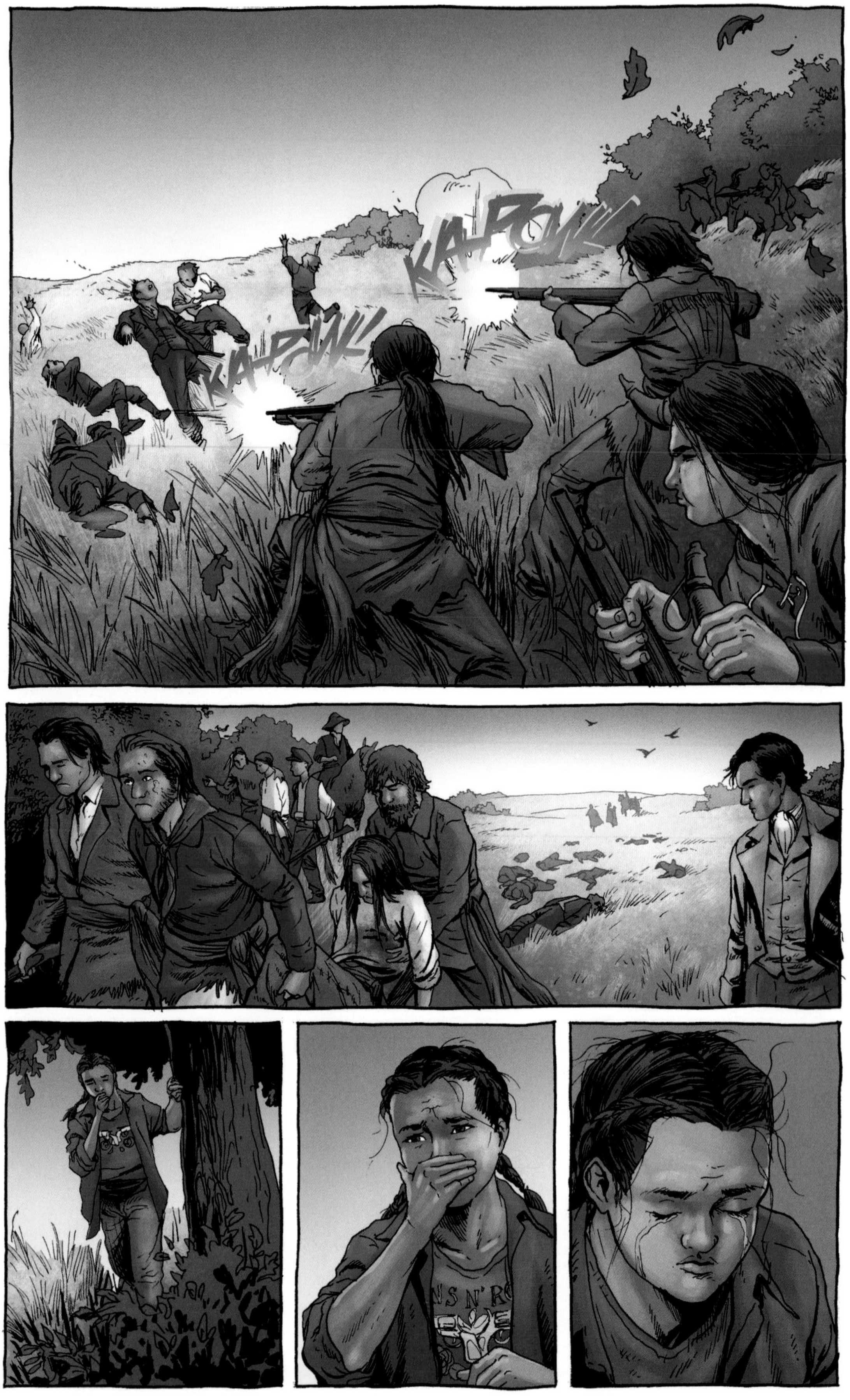
KA-POW!
KA-POW!

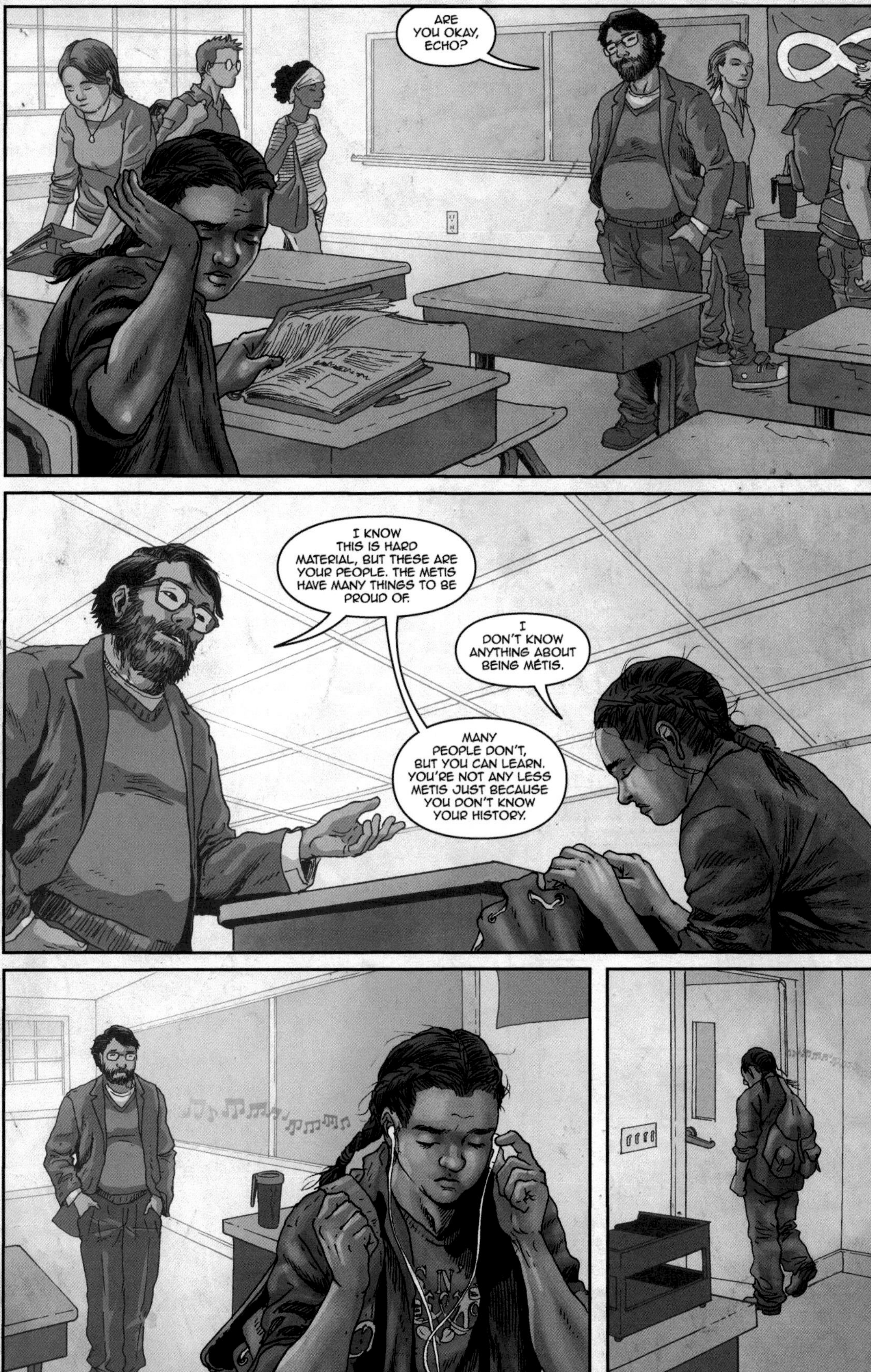
ARE YOU OKAY, ECHO?
I KNOW THIS IS HARD MATERIAL, BUT THESE ARE YOUR PEOPLE. THE METIS HAVE MANY THINGS TO BE PROUD OF.
I DON'T KNOW ANYTHING ABOUT BEING MÉTIS.
MANY PEOPLE DON'T, BUT YOU CAN LEARN. YOU'RE NOT ANY LESS METIS JUST BECAUSE YOU DON'T KNOW YOUR HISTORY.

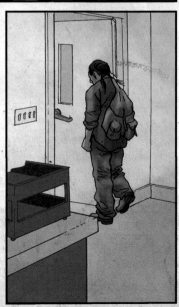

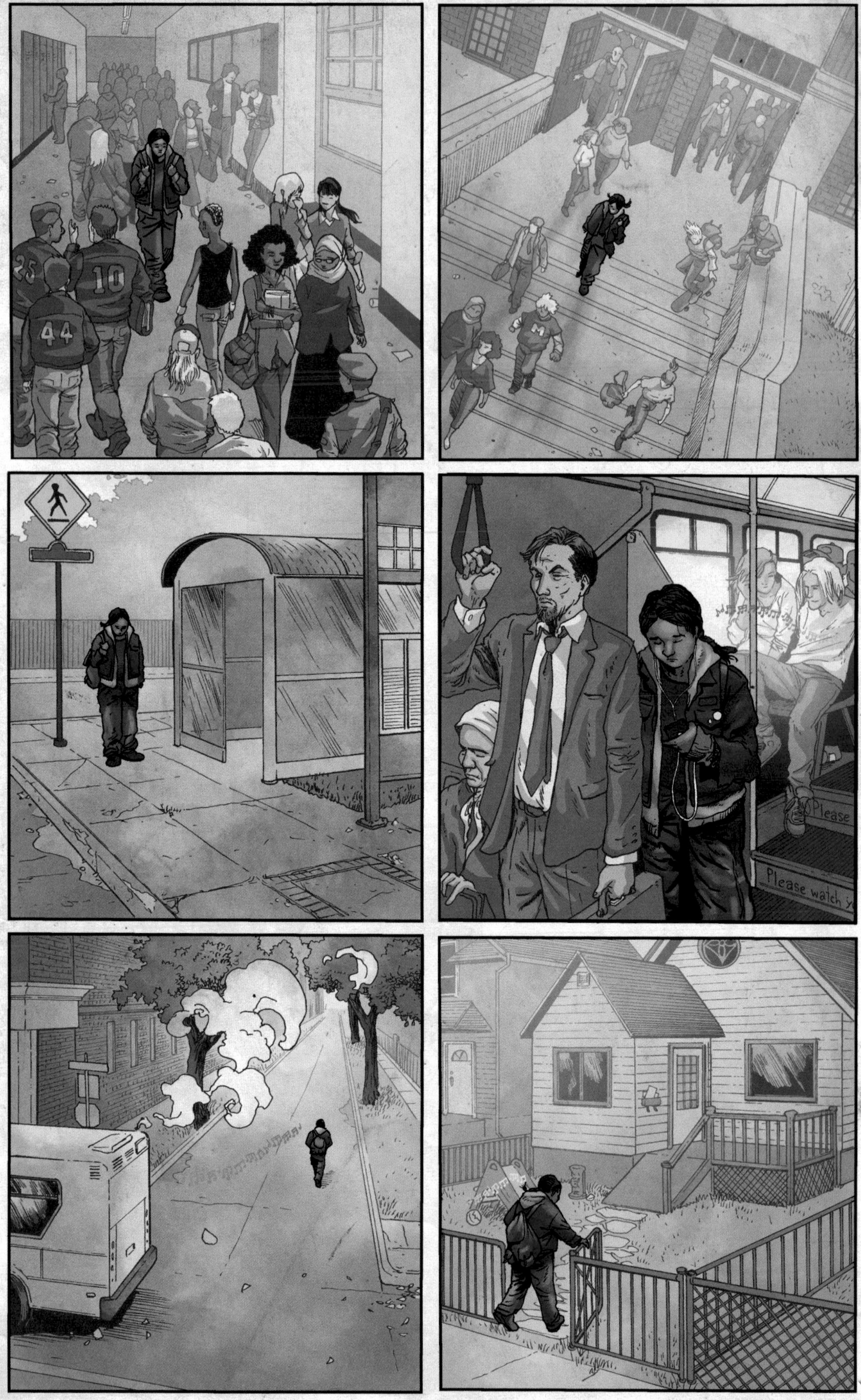
Please
Please watch y

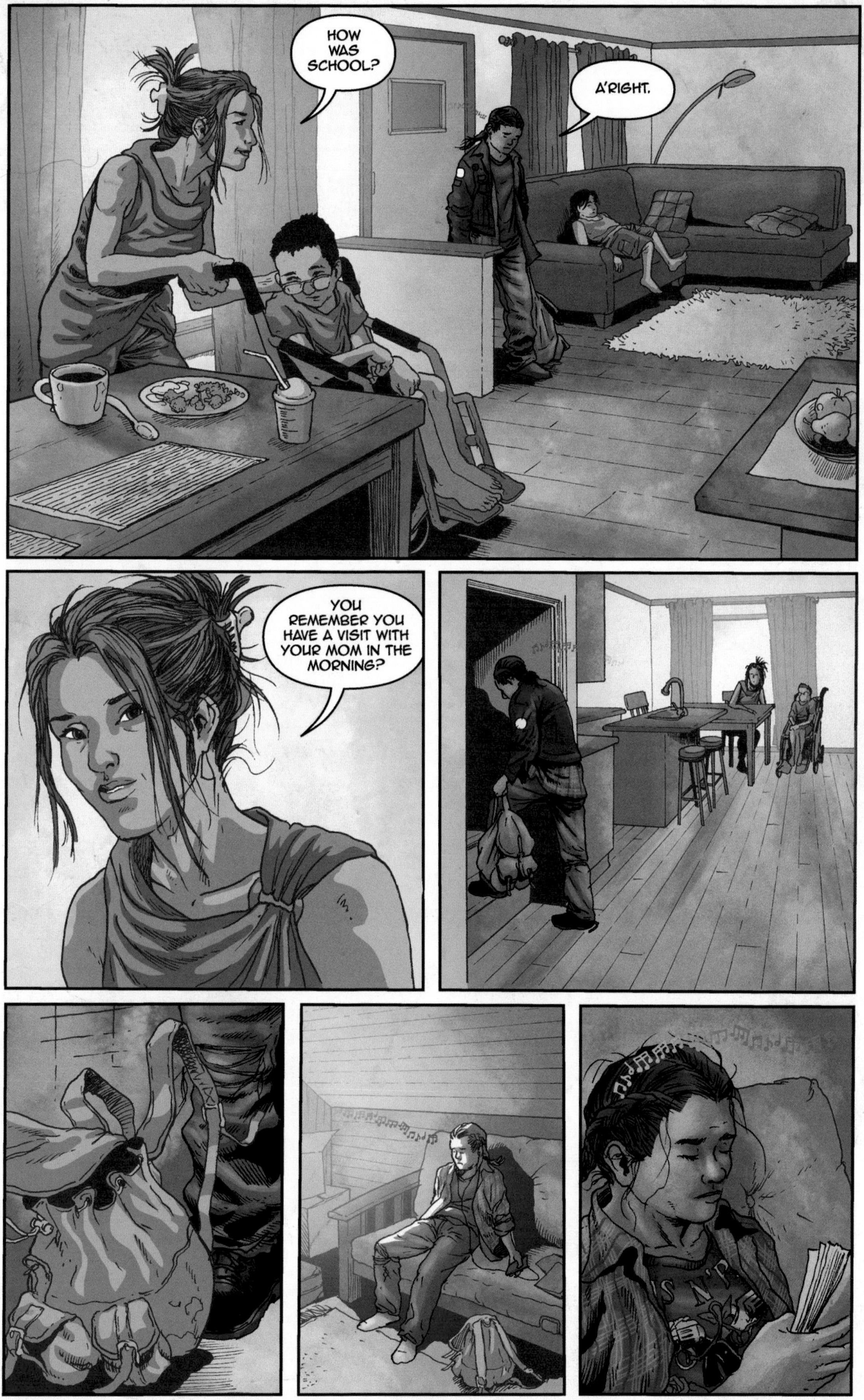
HOW WAS SCHOOL?
A'RIGHT.
YOU REMEMBER YOU HAVE A VISIT WITH YOUR MOM IN THE MORNING?

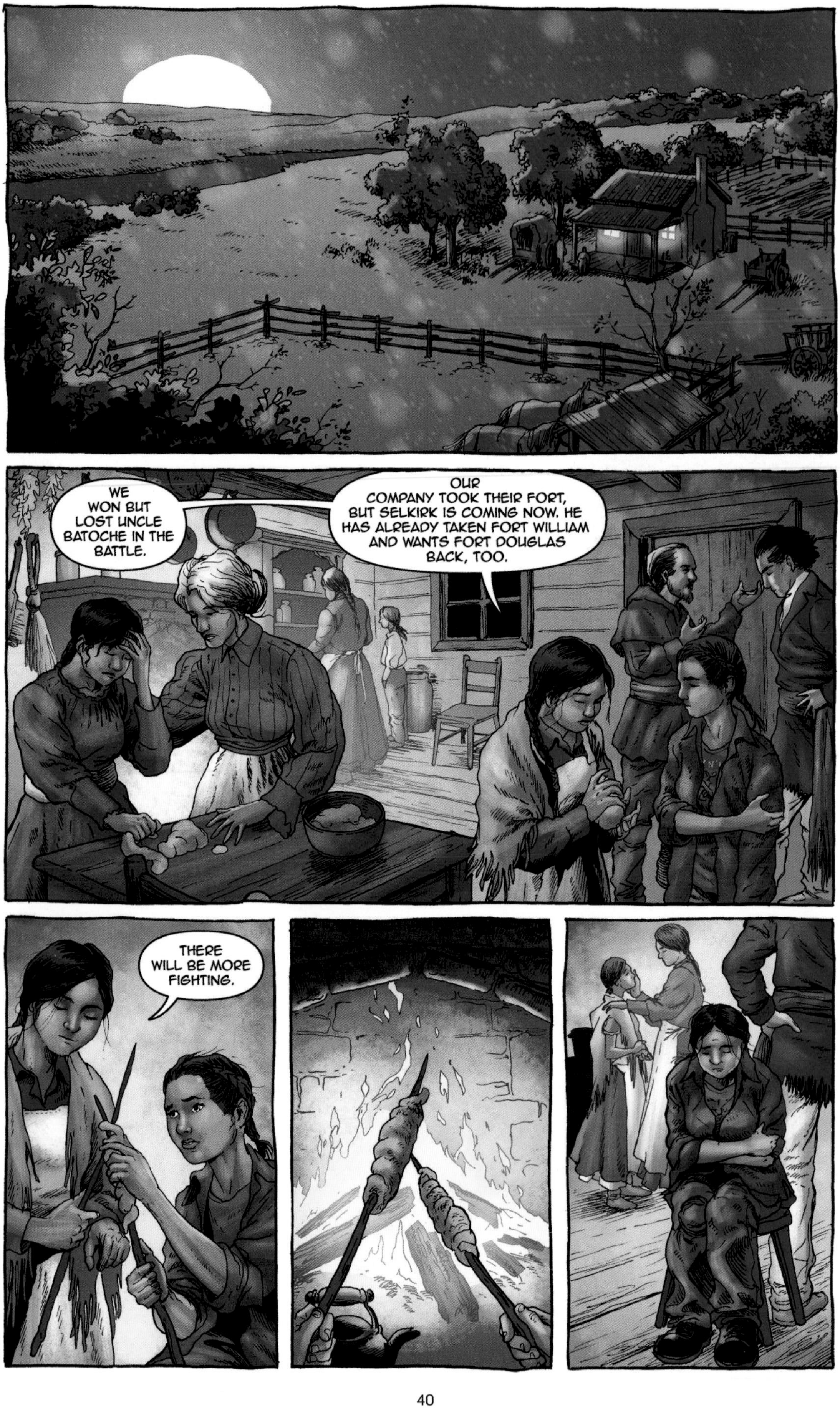
WE WON BUT LOST UNCLE BATOCHE IN THE BATTLE.
OUR COMPANY TOOK THEIR FORT, BUT SELKIRK IS COMING NOW. HE HAS ALREADY TAKEN FORT WILLIAM AND WANTS FORT DOUGLAS BACK, TOO.
THERE WILL BE MORE FIGHTING.

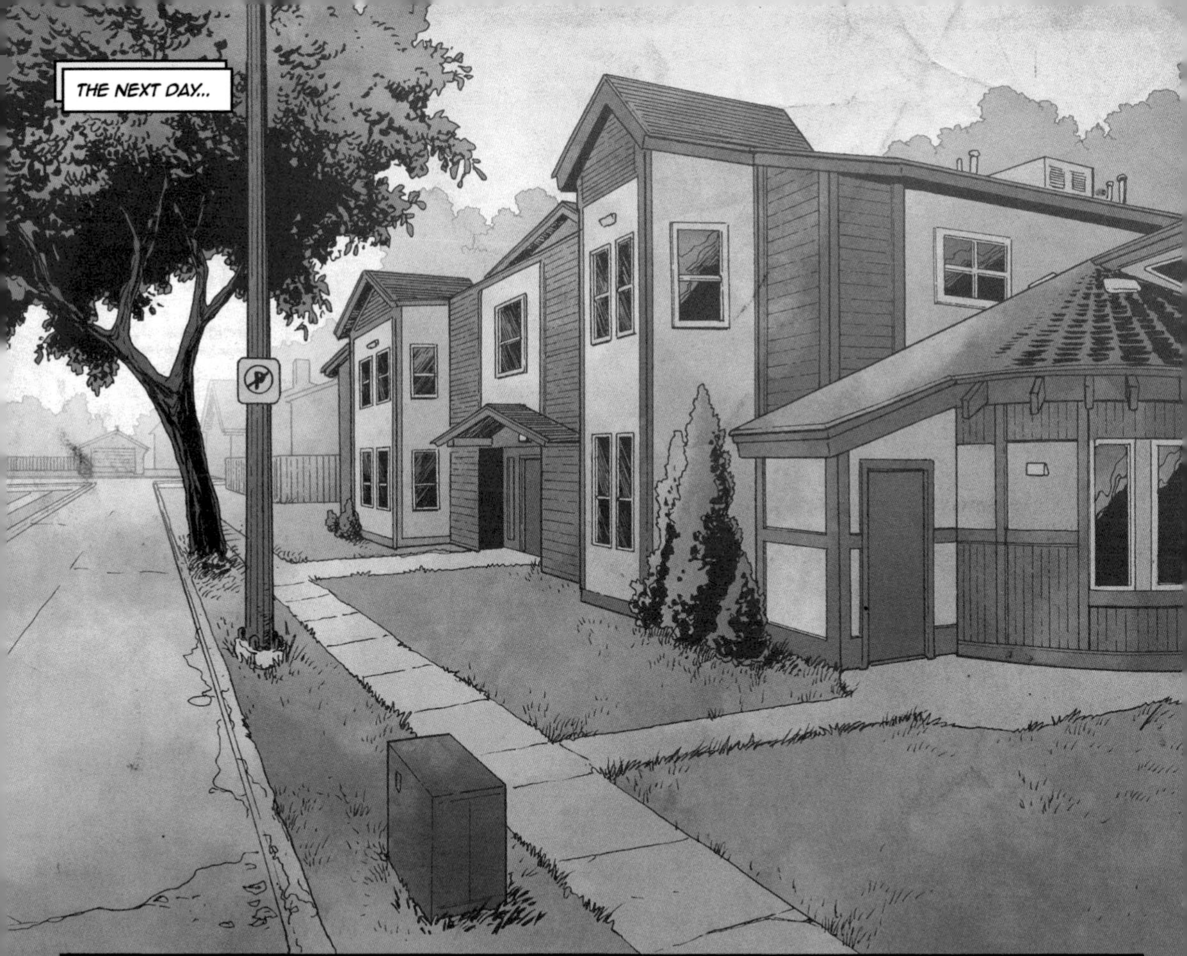
THE NEXT DAY...

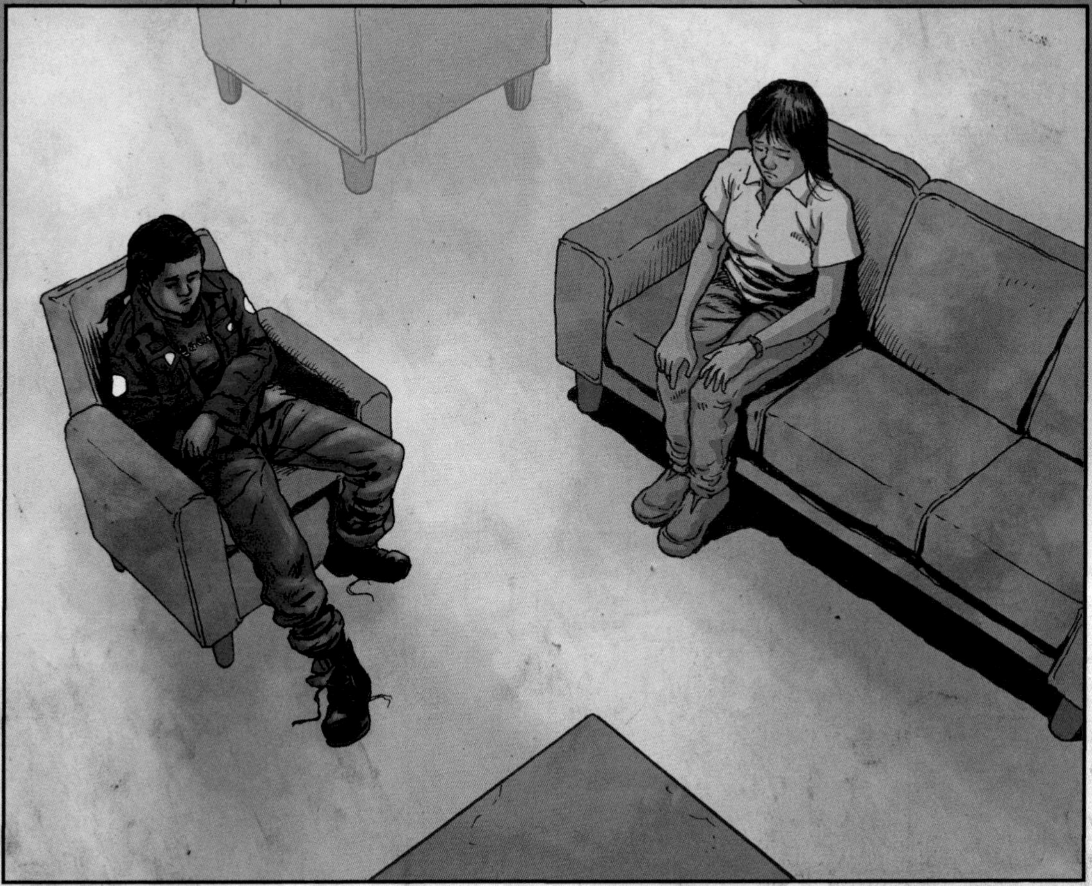

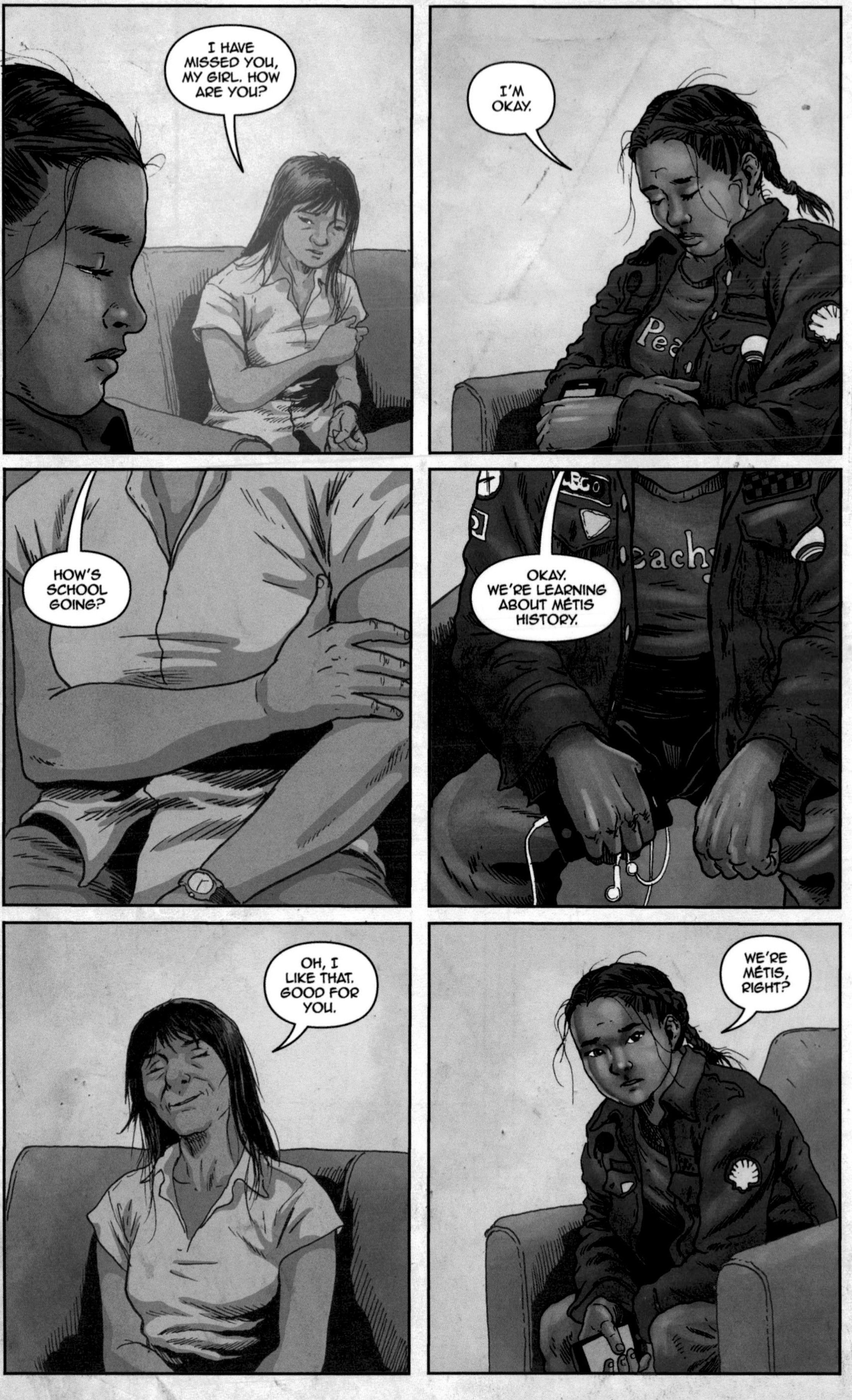
I HAVE MISSED YOU, MY GIRL. HOW ARE YOU?
I'M OKAY.
HOW'S SCHOOL GOING?
OKAY. WE'RE LEARNING ABOUT MÉTIS HISTORY.
OH, I LIKE THAT. GOOD FOR YOU.
WE'RE MÉTIS, RIGHT?

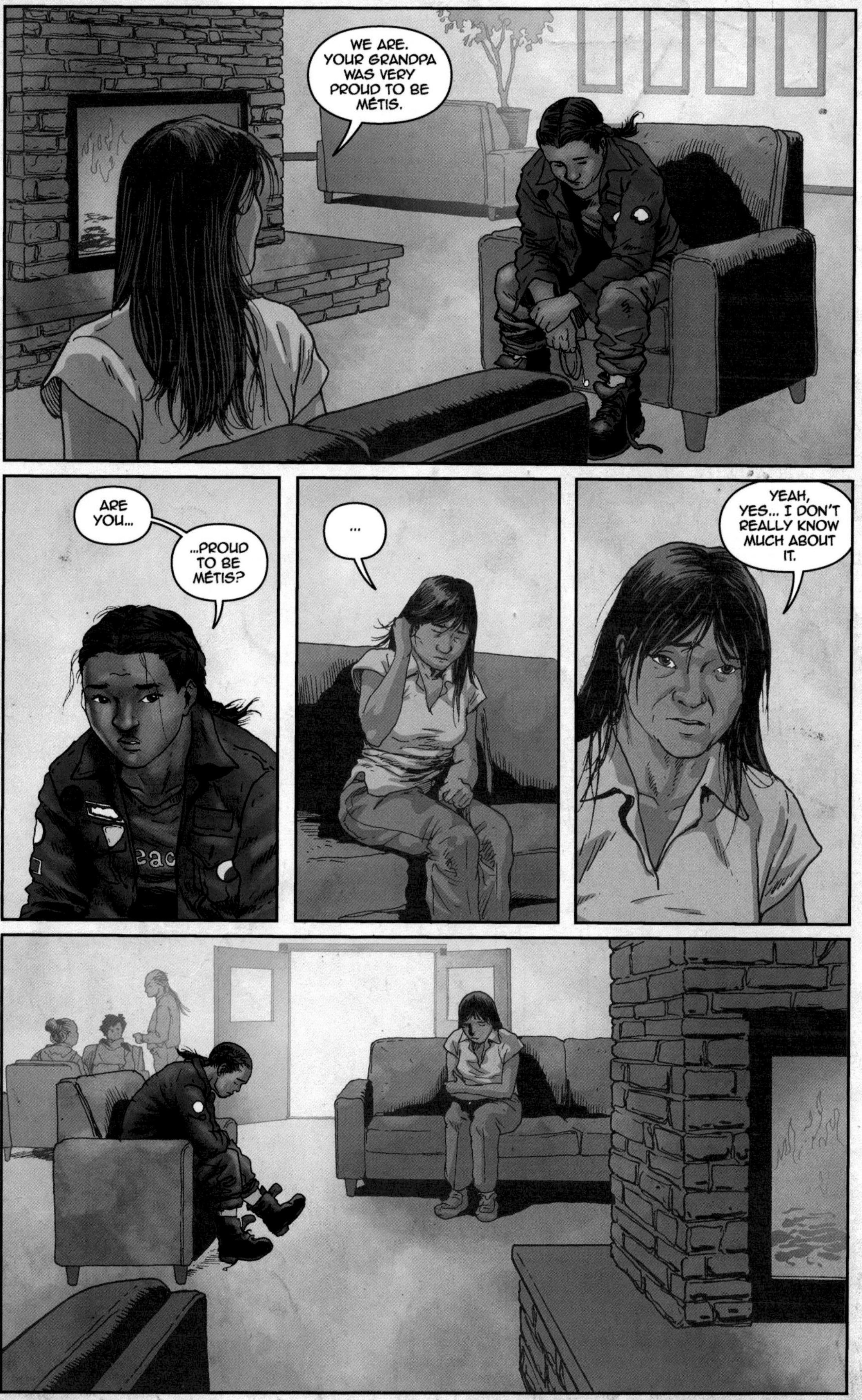
WE ARE. YOUR GRANDPA WAS VERY PROUD TO BE MÉTIS.
ARE YOU...
...PROUD TO BE MÉTIS?
...
YEAH, YES... I DON'T REALLY KNOW MUCH ABOUT IT.

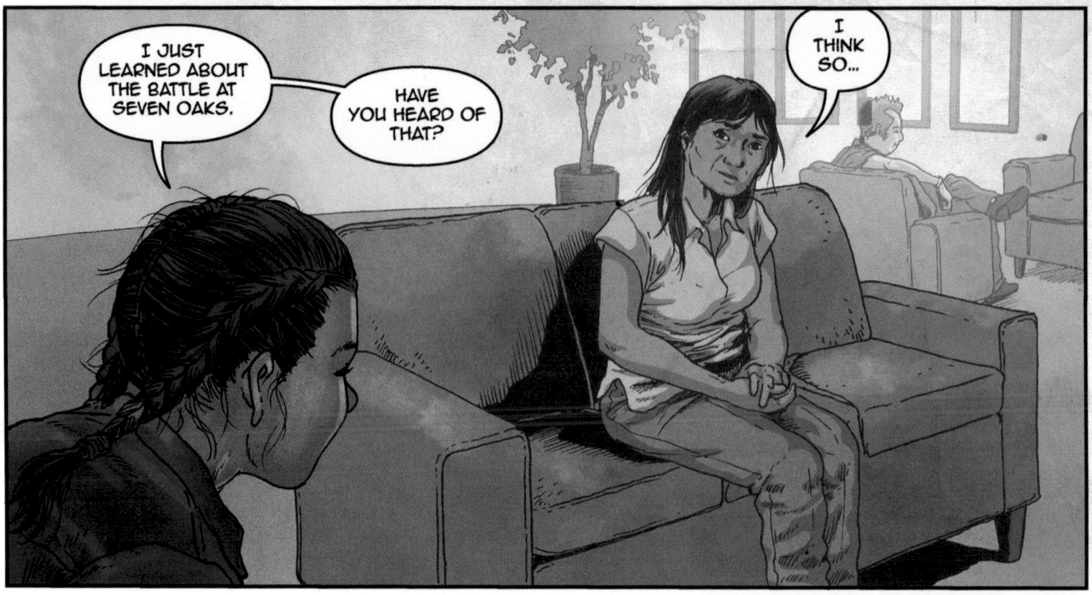
I JUST LEARNED ABOUT THE BATTLE AT SEVEN OAKS.
HAVE YOU HEARD OF THAT?
I THINK SO...

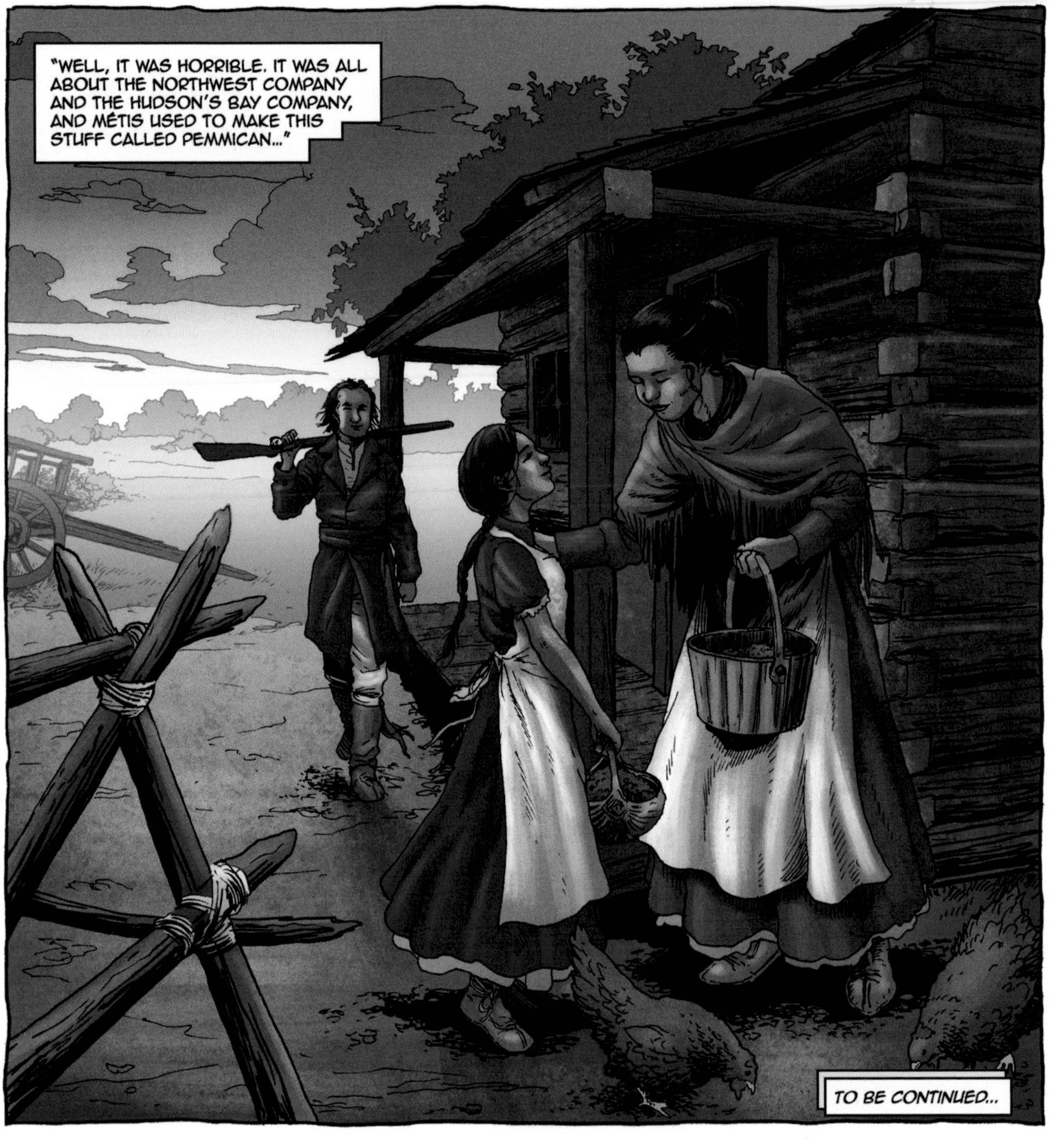
"WELL, IT WAS HORRIBLE. IT WAS ALL ABOUT THE NORTHWEST COMPANY AND THE HUDSON'S BAY COMPANY, AND MÉTIS USED TO MAKE THIS STUFF CALLED PEMMICAN..."
TO BE CONTINUED...

TIMELINE OF THE
PEMMICAN WARS

BEFORE 1806 – The second half of the 18th century was a time of increasing European presence in British North America. Forts and trading posts were built along the major rivers across the west of the continent. The North West Company (NWC), founded in 1779 and headquartered in Montréal, became a fierce rival of the older Hudson's Bay Company (HBC), with both companies vying to control the fur trade.

1809 – The NWC builds Fort Gibraltar where the Red and Assiniboine rivers meet, establishing their dominance of the fur trade in the region.

May 29, 1811 – The Hudson's Bay Company grants 116,000 square miles of land in Rupertsland to The Earl of Selkirk Thomas Douglas, for an "agricultural settlement" (the Selkirk or Red River Settlement) in the District of Assiniboia, which encompassed southern Manitoba and parts of present-day Minnesota, North and South Dakota, Ontario, and Saskatchewan.

Late August, 1812 – The first group of Selkirk Settlers arrives in Red River with the newly-appointed governor, Miles Macdonell, a former officer in the Royal Canadian Volunteers and a friend of Selkirk's.

October 1812 – Another group of Selkirk Settlers arrives at the colony, too late to plant any crops. Members of Chief Peguis's band (Saulteaux) help the settlers survive their first winter and avoid starvation.

January 8, 1814 – Governor Macdonell issues the Pemmican Proclamation, forbidding the export of pemmican and other provisions outside of Assiniboia for a year. He wants to ensure there are enough supplies to feed the settlers; however, the proclamation threatens the survival of local Métis, Indigenous, and European freemen families, who make their living selling pemmican and other supplies to the NWC.

June 1814 – An armed HBC force is sent to the NWC post at Rivière la Souris and breaks into the fort to seize supplies. Eventually the two companies reach an uneasy agreement.

July 1814 – Governor Macdonell forbids hunting bison on horseback because they are being chased too far away for people to hunt on foot.

Fall 1814 – NWC partner Duncan Cameron accuses Governor Macdonell of infringing on the rights of the Métis and freemen by preventing them from hunting on horseback. Macdonell and Cameron continue to plot against each other, and Macdonell attempts to raise a militia from the settlers.

April 17, 1815 – A magistrate issues a warrant for Governor Macdonell's arrest. Macdonell surrenders two months later.

June 11 – 27, 1815 – The Red River colony is attacked by Métis, freemen, and NWC agents, with 40-odd colonists dispersed to Jack River, Norway House, and Pembina. The Métis prepare an address to the Government of Canada asserting their claims to the lands of the Red River.

August 19, 1815 – The colonists return to the colony under the protection of the HBC with several of their agents and clerks.

November 1815 – Robert Semple, a merchant with no political or administrative experience, arrives at the Red River Colony as the HBC's new territorial governor. He is accompanied by another 160 settlers.

June 10, 1816 – On Governor Semple's orders the North West Company's Fort Gibraltar, is dismantled and burned in retaliation for the NWC's attack on the Red River Settlement.

June 18, 1816 – Around 60 Métis and freemen from Portage la Prairie are sent to escort pemmican to boats at Frog Plain/Grenouillière (called Seven Oaks by the Selkirk settlers). They are led by Cuthbert Grant and are ordered to stay away from Fort Douglas, the rebuilt HBC fort.

June 19, 1816 – Men from Fort Douglas spot Grant's party crossing the plains. Governor Semple takes 20 men to meet them, resulting in the Battle of Seven Oaks.

June 22, 1816 – After the Battle of Seven Oaks, Grant and his party capture Fort Douglas, breaking up the colony for a second time. The settlers leave for Lake Winnipeg.

August 13, 1816 – Lord Selkirk and his HBC men capture the NWC's Fort William.

January 10, 1817 – The NWC surrenders Fort Douglas without a fight to Selkirk's forces.

1817 – Cuthbert Grant leaves for Montreal to face charges related to the Battle of Seven Oaks. He is later cleared of all charges.

1818 – William Coltman completes his report on the Battle of Seven Oaks and the events leading up to it, placing the blame on both the Hudson's Bay Company and the North West Company for the events that took place.

1820 – Thomas Douglas, the Earl of Selkirk, dies.

1821 – The NWC and HBC merge into one company.

PEMMICAN

1 kg. of thinly sliced or ground meat: game (moose, deer, caribou), bison, or beef
750 grams of dried berries, such as blueberries, saskatoons, or cranberries
500 grams of lard

1. Preheat oven to 180° F (80° C). Spread meat in a single layer on a baking sheet, and leave to dry for at least eight hours.
2. Grind the meat (Traditionally, the dried meat would be ground between two rocks, but in this case, a food processor or blender could be used). Place in bowl.
3. Grind the fruit. Add to bowl.
4. Melt the lard, then add to above ingredients and mix well. Let cool. Roll into balls or pack into a pan, then cut into squares.
5. Store in a container in a dry place.

BARD OF THE MÉTIS

Pierre Falcon, a North West Company clerk, was best known as a Métis poet and songwriter. Perhaps his best-known song was about the battle at Seven Oaks. Here are the first two verses, in French, as he wrote it, and an English translation.

La Chanson de la Grenouillère

Voulez-vous écouter chanter
Une chanson de vérité?
Le dix-neuf de juin, la bande des Bois-Brûlés
Sont arrivés comme des braves guerriers.
En arrivant à la Grenouillère

Nous avons fait trois prisonniers;
Trois prisonniers des Arkanays
Qui sont ici pour piller notr' pays.

Would you like to hear me sing
Of a true and recent thing?
It was June nineteen, the band of Bois-Brûlés
Arrived that day.
Oh the brave warriors they!

We took three foreigners prisoners when
We came to the place called Frog, Frog Plain.
They were men who'd come from Orkney
Who'd come, you see,
To rob our country.

HighWater Press gratefully acknowledges the financial support of the Province of Manitoba through the Department of Culture, Heritage & Tourism and the Manitoba Book Publishing Tax Credit, and the Government of Canada through the Canada Book Fund (CBF) for our publishing activities.

The publisher also acknowledges the support of the Canada Council for the Arts, which last year invested $153 million to bring the arts to Canadians throughout the country.

Nous remercions le Conseil des arts du Canada de son soutien. L'an dernier, le Conseil a investi 153 millions de dollars pour mettre de l'art dans la vie des Canadiennes et des Canadiens de tout le pays.

 Canada Council   Conseil des Arts
for the Arts   du Canada

Printed and bound in Canada by Friesens
Design by Relish New Brand Experience
Content reviewer: Fred Shore, Department of Native Studies, University of Manitoba

24 23 22 21 20 19 18 17   1 2 3 4 5

Library and Archives Canada Cataloguing in Publication

Vermette, Katherena, 1977-, author
     Pemmican wars / writer, Katherena Vermette ; art, Scott B. Henderson ; colours, Donovan Yaciuk.

(A girl called Echo ; vol. 1)
ISBN 978-1-55379-678-7 (softcover)

     1. Graphic novels. I. Yaciuk, Donovan, 1975-, colourist
II. Henderson, Scott B., illustrator III. Title.
IV. Series: Vermette, Katherena, 1977 . Girl called Echo ; vol. 1

PN6733.V47P46 2017   j741.5'971   C2017-904966-6

www.highwaterpress.com
Winnipeg, Manitoba
Treaty 1 Territory and homeland of the Métis Nation